THE EXTRA MAN

THE EXTRA MAN

E. C. TUBB

WILDSIDE PRESS

Copyright © 1954 by E.C. Tubb; copyright © 2011 by Lisa John.
Published by Wildside Press LLC.
wildsidepress.com | bcmystery.com

CHAPTER I

From the gentle slope of the foothills Poker Flats stretched like a frozen sea beneath the cold light of a near-full Moon. Shadows blotched the surface, black pools against the grey-white, thrown from swelling dunes and wind-blown rock, collecting in ebon patches and inky channels, etching the unevenness of the desert. They made an odd pattern those shadows, an irregular polka-dot pattern of light and dark, strange, a little alien; almost disturbing in the deep silence of the night.

Watching them, Curt Rosslyn could almost imagine that he was no longer on Earth.

He leaned against a crumbling boulder, a slim man, not tall, not heavily built, but with a litheness and easiness of movement that betrayed hidden strength. Behind him the mountains reared their jagged crests against the star-shot sky, and far out across the wastes of Poker Flats, dim lights gleamed for an instant, gleamed and died like the fading embers of forgotten hope.

He sighed a little, his grey eyes clouded with dreams as he stared at the shadowed desert and the worn mountains. Mars was something like this, he reflected. And the airless craters of the Moon, and the distant sun-scorched Mercury. He sighed again, tilting his head and staring up towards the burning glory of the heavens, idly tracing the well-remembered constellations.

The Big Dipper, Polaris the Pole Star, and the sprawling length of Draco. The regular shape of Cassiopeia and the angular shape of Andromeda with its misty nebula. Cross-shaped Bootes, and the scintillating cluster of the Pleiades. Glowing Formalhaut, and the splendour of Vega. Low on the horizon Rigel and Betelgeux blazed in the glory of Orion, warning of the winter to come, and above all, glowing like a tracery of shimmering gems, the heart-stopping splendour of the Milky Way.

He knew them all, had known them for as long as he could remember, and the familiar constellations felt like old friends. He had squinted at them through the lenses of his first crude telescope. Then, after many weary hours, he had stared at them with the aid of a hand-ground mirror and the extra power of his six-inch reflector had opened new worlds of glory. He had seen the satellites of Jupiter, the transit of Venus and Mercury, studied the sands of Mars and walked in imagination on the surface of the Moon. The Moon! He smiled up at it, winking at the splotched face of the satellite, then, obeying the warning of finely-tuned reflexes, turned and stared over the desert.

Light and sound came towards him.

Twin streamers of brilliance stabbed across the desert, dispelling the shadows and ruining the alien atmosphere with the harsh reality of commonsense. The headlights swung and dipped, rose towards the stars and veered from rock and heaped dunes of arid sand. With the approach of the headlights the sound of the jeep sent flat echoes from the age-old heights of the mountains, and Curt sighed, relaxing against his boulder.

"Rosslyn?"

"Yes." Curt straightened and stepped towards the vehicle. "Comain?"

"That's right." A tall, lean, almost emaciated figure unfolded itself from behind the wheel and in the starlight Curt could see the pale face and thick lensed spectacles of his friend. "Time to go back, Curt. I volunteered to collect you, the driver was busy winning a thousand dollar pot."

"I could have waited." Curt stared at the stars again, almost forgetting that he was no longer alone. "Beautiful aren't they?"

"Yes." Something in the tall man's voice made Curt glance at him, then look away. "They're clean and bright and wonderful, Curt—and they're waiting. New worlds, new peoples, new ideals and cultures. New frontiers, Curt, and we're on the threshold of opening the way for everyone."

"Perhaps, but it won't be for a long time yet."

"No, Curt. The first step is always the hardest. First we have to create a system of space travel that can be used by private firms and entrepreneurs, and not just national Space Agencies that are tools of the military. To put it on the same basis as commercial airlines. Once we have done that the rest must follow. The exploitation of the vast resources of the solar system. The questions of the legal ownership of extra-terrestrial minerals and resources will have a seismic effect on selfish nationalistic interests and boundaries. A new world view, with the harvests of outer space being used for the good of all mankind. It may take time, Curt, but it will be done."

The tall man fell silent as he stared at the brilliant face of the near-full Moon. Taller than Curt, stoop shouldered, thin-faced and weak-eyed, yet his high forehead and large skull told of the intelligence residing in his ungainly body. His hands were thin and slender, the fingers long and supple, the hands of an artist, an idealist, a dreamer. Ambition burned within him, not the normal ambition of the majority of men, for wealth meant nothing to him, but the relentless ambition of the scholar. He was driven by the twin devils of curiosity and speculation. He wondered, and he built, then wondered again and built afresh. He would never stop until his eyes closed in the final sleep. He was that kind of man.

A thin wind blew across the desert, stirring the sand a little and chilling their blood. Curt shivered, then, as if ashamed of himself, tried to ignore the warnings of his body.

"Better get back," said Comain quietly. "You don't want to catch a cold now."

"I won't."

"You shivered and it's getting colder." Comain started towards the jeep. "Come on, Curt."

Curt fell into step with the tall man and their feet scuffed against the desert as they walked towards the silent jeep. "You know, Comain, with all those gadgets you built, all I have to do is to press buttons. Those things you fitted should be able to operate the ship on their own."

"The servo mechanisms?" Comain smiled. "They will help but they can only do what you direct them to do. The final decision must be yours."

He halted by the side of the jeep and folded his long body behind the wheel. Curt sat beside him, then, as they began jolting over the desert, clung to the metal frame of the windscreen.

"Actually," he said above the whine of the engine. "I should have thought it possible to build a robot pilot for the first test flight. Could you do that?"

"Yes." Comain stared before him, his weak eyes narrowed a little as he steered the vehicle over the undulating sand. He wasn't deceived, and yet he felt grateful to Curt for easing his inner pain. They had grown up together, sharing their boyhood, discovering the stars and the mysteries of science at the same time. Both had dreamed the same dreams, weaving impossible worlds of romantic mystery with their youthful imaginations. They had argued, built, planned; even fought a little. They had helped each other, and, as the years passed, had grown closer even than brothers.

But now they had to part.

Little things had decided it. Weak eyes against perfect vision. Weight against weight, height against height, reflex against reflex. They had been tested, examined, checked—and Curt had won.

Comain had known it for more than five years now. He had watched his body, his frail, stooped, weak body, and he had known. Ambition had not died with the knowledge but had been channeled into a different path. Not for him the glories of space, but, science covered a wide field and cybernetics was something in which he could take a keen interest. And so he had turned to the design of more and more efficient machines. Small and compact, with built-in relays and predictable response to external stimuli. He had designed the controls for the spaceship, the things of metal that could operate faster, better, than the muscles of any man.

And yet his hurt had been deep and something of the old pain still lingered.

"I could build a mechanical pilot," he said. "I could build one better than any man, but we're up against weight limitations, Curt, and no machine now known can do what a man can do within that limitation."

"Good." Curt grinned with a flash of white teeth. "I don't care what you do later, Comain, but I'm glad that you've had to admit defeat now. I've looked forward to this for a long time and I'd hate for you to replace me with a thing of steel and computer chips."

"No chance of that." Comain swung the wheel as he guided the jeep around a jagged mound of rock. "Although we've had space travel for many years now, there is still much to be learned about what happens to a man out there, and how he can cope with the new space technologies we are pioneering. You're a guinea pig, Curt, my day will come after they address the problem that the average human body can't stand high G without damage. Then we'll have ships with the passengers in acceleration tanks and robots at the controls."

"Maybe." Curt grunted as the vehicle bounced and jarred his teeth. "How's your research going on the Great Idea?"

"The predictor?" The thin man shrugged. "It'll come, Curt, it will have to come. Faster and better computers will be built. One day they'll realise that a machine able to absorb information and then to predict probable events from that information will be essential if we are to advance this civilisation of ours." His thin lips twisted cynically as he stared at the desert before him. "Probably the next war will do it."

"You think that there'll be one?"

"I do. Every thinking man does. We've managed to negotiate an uneasy peace but the weapons are ready, the men are waiting, and the same tensions still exist. War will come, Curt, it can't be avoided, and, in a way, it could be a good thing."

"A good thing! Are you crazy?"

"No. Look at it this way, Curt. Each war has brought rapid scientific advancement. The First World War brought the development of flight, the advancement of surgery, the use of strange machines. The second brought the jet engine, the atomic bomb, the proximity fuse. The third..." He shrugged. "Who knows? We may all die from the alphabet bombs but if we don't we may stumble on something quite new."

"The predictor?"

"Naturally, but I didn't mean that. The predictor isn't new, and it will come, war or no war. I mean something different, new, perhaps something not even imagined yet."

He grunted as the jeep bounced over the edge of a wide road and with a sweep of his hand disengaged the low register. The swaying headlights steadied as they spun along the smooth road and the flickering hand of the speedometer crawled across the dial as the thin man trod on the throttle.

"The Colonel was furious at your taking off like that," he explained above the rush of displaced air. "I tried to tell him how you felt but he didn't seem to understand."

"The Colonel has no imagination." Curt stared up at the brilliant Moon. "Sometimes a man just has to get off somewhere by himself. Sometimes he just can't stand people fussing around him." He looked at the thin man. "Can you understand what I mean?"

"I understand." Comain thinned his lips as he nodded, then, taking one hand from the wheel, pointed ahead. "There she is!"

Light blazed before them. Light and the delicate tracery of a high wire fence. The squat bulk of a tracking station loomed on their left, the white and red warning notices ringing the area showed stark on their right, and before them…

It towered like the delicate spire from some ancient dream. Smooth, glistening with streamlined perfection, needle-pointed and resting on its wide fins. Loading platforms and gantries clustered around it, but even their bulk couldn't hide the sheer beauty of the man-made thing resting in the centre of the area. It seemed to hover on the levelled sand, like a thing without weight or substance. It soared towards the beckoning stars and the lights ringing the area shimmered in scintillating ripples from the gleaming hull.

A spaceship.

Curt stared at it as he had stared at it a million times in imagination and in reality. For him it was the final realisation of ambition, the solid proof that he was not living in a dream. Before him rose the spaceship, real, solid, fact. A dream made tangible, a thing of ten thousand hopes and eternal longing from countless men crystallized into something that would open up the road to the stars for the many and not just for the few.

And he was its pilot.

Guards stepped forward as the jeep droned towards the high wire fence and Comain grunted as his foot moved from accelerator to brake. Lights blazed at him, forcing him to squint and shield his weak eyes, then, recognised by the guards, they droned into the wired area and towards the low bulk of the living quarters.

"Better go straight to bed if you want to dodge the Colonel," he suggested. "Anyway, you could do with some sleep."

"I can't sleep." Curt twisted in his seat as he stared at the towering space ship. "Man! How can I sleep? This is it, Comain! This is what I've wanted all my life! I blast at dawn and you talk of sleep!"

"Dawn?" The thin man frowned as he glanced at his left wrist. "In four hours?"

"Is it?" Curt shrugged. "I'm not wearing a watch. Zero hour is at dawn—that's all I care about."

"Then what are you going to do?"

"I don't know. Walk about perhaps, yarn with the boys, play poker, anything. Don't you realise that this is my last night on Earth? Tomorrow I'll be in space, swinging around the Moon watching the naked stars, feeling what it's like to be in free fall. I want to enjoy all this while I can. I've no time for sleep."

"Don't talk like that. Curt." Comain swallowed, then grinned as he brought the jeep to a halt. "Don't talk as if this were your last night alive I mean. You'll be coming back. You know you will, and when you do, you'll be a hero. Think of it. Curt. The first space pilot to have circled the Moon in an independently piloted craft! Your name will be in every history book from now on."

"Perhaps, but Comain, it won't be the same after this. Nothing will. This is all I've lived for and once I've done it, what then? Can I bear to settle down again? From a personal standpoint, this is my last night on Earth and I'll be damned if I waste it in sleep."

Lithely the slender man swung from his seat then stood looking down at Comain.

"What are you going to do?"

"Check the radio gear again I suppose. You know that I'll be in contact with you all the time?"

"Yes."

"I'll be seeing you at dawn then." Comain narrowed his eyes as he saw a tall, trimly uniformed figure emerge from one of the low huts. "Better watch it if you don't want to see the Colonel. He's just left his quarters."

"Has he?" Curt grinned and moved away from the jeep. "I can do without his company for now. Be seeing you, Comain." He lifted his arm in a casual salute and walked rapidly from the vehicle, the shadows between the glaring arc lights hiding him from view.

Comain nodded, not answering, then, with a strangely bitter expression on his thin features, sat hugging the wheel and staring towards the glistening perfection of the waiting rocket ship. He didn't answer the Colonel when Adams spoke to him. He didn't seem to notice the chill wind sweeping from the desert or the fading light of the burning stars. He just sat waiting, his weak eyes clouded with thought and his stooped body lax behind the wheel.

Waiting for dawn.

CHAPTER II

Dawn came with a thin wind, a chill wind bearing promise of early winter and carrying a fine dust of stinging sand. In the east a pink glow suffused the sky and a scud of thin cloud hid the dying light of the fading stars. The Moon had gone, falling below the horizon, and it was strange to see men glancing to where it had been, even though they knew that the ship would be aimed at a set of co-ordinates rather than a visual target.

Adams gathered them all in the control room for a final briefing.

The Colonel showed signs of strain, his eyes were bloodshot and his grizzled hair rumpled, matching his usually impeccable uniform. He glared at Curt, almost as if he would like to give the young man hell for slipping away from his surveillance, then, as he stared at the young man, shrugged and got down to business.

"Blast-off's in one hour," he said abruptly. "The ship has been fueled, the instruments checked, and the weather report is favourable. You will each report in turn."

"Tracking stations standing by, sir."

"Radio checked and ready." Comain leaned against the edge of the table and winked at Curt.

"Medical examination completed." The doctor yawned and rubbed his tired eyes. "Is all this necessary, Adams? I can't see why I've got to stand by. There's nothing more I can do until Rosslyn returns."

"You've given him the drugs?"

"Yes. The complete hell-brew. Stuff to lower his instinctive muscular resistance to strain. Other stuff to prevent congealing of his blood." The doctor looked at Curt. "Be careful of that by the way. If you cut yourself you're liable to bleed to death."

"If I'm injured I take the green injection. Right?"

"Right." The doctor yawned again. "Damn it all, Adams! I'm an old man, I need my sleep. Can I go now?"

"You are excused, doctor," said the Colonel stiffly. "Naturally you will make no attempt to leave the area."

"And miss the chance of almost taking a man apart?" The doctor grinned at Curt. "Man! Wait until you see what I've got lined up for you when you return. Three hundred tests and twenty days of controlled feeding. I'll make you wish that you had never gone."

"It'll be worth it." Curt grinned after the old medico as he left the room. "Rocket checked O.K.?"

A technician nodded. "Yeah. I examined the venturis myself. The ship won't let you down, Rosslyn."

"I hope not," said Curt quietly. "There won't be any chance of repairing it if it does."

"It won't let you down." Adams jerked his head and the technician left the room. "Now. You, Comain will keep in constant radio communication with the ship. You, Rosslyn, will maintain a running commentary on everything that happens. I mean that literally, Rosslyn. I want you to keep talking, about the ship, your own reactions, even your thoughts and emotions. I don't want you to freeze up on us. This thing has cost too much for a temperamental pilot to queer things. You may die, you know that, but if you do I want to know just why. Remember that no matter what happens to you another ship will be coming after. There will be other men, lots of them, and you may help to save their lives."

"I understand, Adams."

"I hope that you do." The Colonel sighed and rubbed at his bloodshot eyes. "I want you to come back to us, Rosslyn, alive and well. You know that, so take good care of yourself will you?" He grinned and Curt felt himself warm to the grizzled man.

"I'll take care," he promised. "I…" He paused as a man's voice echoed from a speaker against the wall.

"Zero minus fifty."

"That's it!" Adams heaved himself from his chair. "Get to the ship, Rosslyn. They'll dress you in your anti-G suit there. Comain! Get to your radio and check everything. Move now."

It was psychology of course. A deliberate leaving of everything until the last few minutes when, in the final rush of activity, strain and nervous anticipation would be forgotten.

Curt almost ran from the room, piling into a waiting jeep and feeling the cold wind tug at his hair as he was driven to the base of the loading platform.

Men grabbed him as the vehicle skidded to a halt. They stripped him, dressed him in a one-piece undersuit of non-conducting nylon, then in a thick armour of canvas and plastic.

Swiftly the loading platform carried both Curt and his helpers to the nose of the rocket, and within what seemed an incredibly short time he sat in his padded control chair, the inflated sections of his G-suit pressing hard against his body, his hands, gloved and steady, reaching for the warm-up switches.

"Good luck, Rosslyn!" The last of his helpers grinned as he crawled through the tiny entrance port, swinging the panel behind him and dogging it tight against the rubber gaskets.

Abruptly the radio droned into life.

"Curt. All set?"

"Yes."

"Good. Routine check now. Ready?"

"Fire away."

"Oxygen bottles?"

"Check."

"Drugs?"

"Check."

"Water?" The calm voice of Comain droned on, forcing Curt to keep his mind on the vital supplies of the ship, checking every item, not through fear of any last-minute error, but to keep the pilot's mind from what was coming. Softly, over the calm monotony of Comain;s voice, Curt heard the time signal whispered from some distant speaker.

"Zero minus seven minutes."

Seven minutes!

Four hundred and twenty seconds before he would feel the thunder of the venturis and feel the bone-jarring thrust of acceleration pressure. Seven minutes before he would rise on wings of flame, rise on the thundering power of unleashed energy, rise towards the stars. Sweat oozed from his forehead and he felt an insane desire to stop the whole thing, to get up from his padded chair, open the hatch, return to the safe, sure world of normal men.

"Curt!"

Comain's voice jerked him back to sanity and he licked his lips as he tried to still the butterflies crawling in his stomach. "Yes?"

"What's the matter, getting nervous?"

"A little," he admitted. "How much longer?"

"Take it easy, you'll know when it's time." Curt could almost see his friend's thin features, the thin lips curved in a cynical smile. "Last instructions, Curt. You know what you must do."

"I know. Practically nothing at all."

"That's right. The take-off will be automatic. The gyroscopes will take care of the course. You just sit there and do nothing unless something goes haywire. You'll circle the Moon, the cameras are automatic too, but you'd better check them just in case."

"Just a passenger aren't I?"

"No. Don't make that mistake, Curt. You've got to watch everything all the time, we just don't know what free radiation will do to the instruments, and remember, you've got to land the ship too."

"A parachute could do that."

"Perhaps, you've got one anyway, but it isn't as simple as that, Curt. You are as much an instrument as anything else aboard. On you will rest, in the final analysis, the whole success or failure of this flight. An instrument could fail, the acceleration shock could do it, and you must be there to take its place."

Curt smiled at the radio, grateful to Comain for easing his nervous tension. A whisper came from the radio, the sound of the time check, and over it Curt heard Comain's expression of annoyance.

"Shut that thing off."

"How long, Comain?" Curt licked his dry lips. "How long damn you!"

"Take it easy, Curt. You've got a long time yet."

"You're a liar, Comain. Tell me. How long?" The whispering of the time check gave the answer.

"Zero minus one minute."

One minute!

It was too much. It was impossible for any man born of woman not to dwell on the passing seconds. Later perhaps, when space flight was as normal as catching a plane, the time wouldn't matter so much, but now…

Curt could feel his heart thudding against his ribs as he waited for the rocket to thunder into strident life. Now there was no turning back. Now he just had to sit there, poised over five hundred tons of one of the most violent explosives known, waiting for it to ignite and hurl him beyond the planet of his birth. He would rise on that thundering pillar of flame, rise up and up, through the clouds and through the thinning atmosphere. Up and out—into what?

Space was a void, a vacuum in which the planets swum like lonely fish in an ebon sea. Without temperature, without any heat or light of its own, without gravity, illumined by the faint dots of the distant stars and the naked furnace of the roaring sun. Space was emptiness—or was it? Radiation streamed through that void. The broken atoms of incredible cataclysms, cosmic rays, tides of free electrons, gas, gamma and alpha radiation, and other strange and unguessed at forces. Men had always been protected from them, shielded by the ozone belt of the Heaviside layer, but he was going beyond that protection, venturing his soft and helpless body into the surging currents of outer space.

He could go blind. He could return a distorted cripple, his cells and bones twisted and warped by that flood of radiation. His mind could yield and raving insanity replace his schooled calm. Anything could happen. Anything.

He half rose from the padded seat, his gloved hands fumbling at his harness, the sweat of fear trickling down his face, stinging his eyes and wetting his parched lips with the salty taste of terror.

Comain's voice from the radio jerked him back to sanity.

"Curt! Blast-off in ten seconds. Rockets now warming up."

A mutter echoed throughout the ship. A quivering vibration singing along the metal of the hull, the internal stanchions, sending little ringing sounds from the plastic faces of the instruments and the thin sheeting of the control bank. Curt tensed, then, accepting the inevitable, lost his fear and refastened his harness. Swiftly he scanned the dials, snapping quick reports into the radio.

"Temperature rising. Number four jet higher than the other six. Vibration increasing. How's she look, Contain?"

"Beautiful!" Envy tinged the thin man's reply. "I wish I was with you, Curt."

"So do I," said the slender man feelingly, then gripped the arms of his chair as the muttering grew louder. "Switch in the radio-clock, Comain. I..." He bit his lip as the sound of the rockets rose to a screaming whine, and again he could taste the salt of his own fear.

The whistling roar grew louder, shrieking with the full power of a million tormented giants, yelling a brutal challenge towards the far horizon and the careless stars. Vibration sang from the metal of hull and stanchions, a thin shrilling of jarred atoms, ringing and blending with the pulsing thunder of the blasting rockets. Dimly, over the hell of blasting sound, Curt heard the thin voice from the radio.

"Good luck, Curt. This is it!"

"Yes," he breathed. "Here we go."

Weight slammed at him, thrusting him deep into the padding of his chair, piling tons of invisible lead on chest and stomach, squeezing his lungs and pressing his head down between his shoulders. The weight grew, became a nightmare of ceaseless struggle, a pain-shot, timeless period of eternal anguish.

Blood streamed from his nose and ears, filled his eyes, thundered from his labouring heart and filled his mouth with salty wetness. He gasped, writhing on his padded chair, twisting in the confines of his inflated G-suit and wishing that he were dead. Nothing he had ever experienced had ever been like this. It seemed as if his very bones would protrude through his skin, the flesh ripped away by the piling weight of acceleration pressure. He wanted to black-out, and, same time, fought against it. He wanted to stop the ship, to get out and to call the whole thing off, and at the same time he urged the rockets to still greater thrust, knowing the sooner the ship reached escape velocity the sooner his torment would be over.

The rockets died, cutting with an almost savage abruptness and in the silence little sounds seemed to have gained greater power. The soft hiss of air from an oxygen cylinder, the and rustle of still-vibrating stanchions, the throb and pulse of surging current, and, above all, the muted chatter of the Geiger counter measuring the flood of radiation penetrating the vessel.

Curt stirred, licking his lips and lifting himself into a more comfortable position before the banked controls. His face felt wet, sticky and uncomfortable, stiff and a little numb. Clumsily he unbuckled his mask and dabbed at his features with his gloved hand. He winced at the touch, his muscle and skin feeling as though he had been beaten with a rubber hose, then stared blankly at his gloved fingers.

They were stained with blood.

The radio crackled, and a voice, blurred with static and distorted with emotion echoed from the speaker.

"Curt! Are you all right, Curt? Curt! Answer me!"

He ignored it, unbuckling the safety harness, and even though he had expected it, the eerie sensation of free fall made him catch at the back of the chair in sudden fear. He hovered there, weightless, his feet unsupported and his whole body drifting lightly like a gas-filled balloon, and, as he hovered, smiled.

He didn't need to glance out of the ports at the ebon night of space. He didn't need the sight of the scintillant stars, bright and burning with their cold white fire against the soft velvet of the void. He knew.

He was in space.

CHAPTER III

The room was heavy with coiling clouds of stale smoke and rank with the taste of air which had been breathed too often. It seemed that every man who could possibly find an excuse for cramming himself in the room had done so, and they leaned against the walls, poised on the edges of tables and chairs, smoking, breathing, their eyes heavy with lack of sleep and nervous tension.

Adams sprawled in a chair, his tunic unbuttoned, his grizzled hair rumpled and his bloodshot eyes dull as he listened to the voice of the thin man sitting before the radio. Comain wiped his lips with the back of his hand, adjusted a control a trifle, and leaned closer to the microphone.

"Curt. Comain here. Answer me, Curt. Answer me damn you!"

"Maybe the radio went?" A man whispered the suggestion, then recoiled at the naked hate in Comain's eyes.

"No! That radio was tested up to fifty G. It couldn't have gone. Anyway, the signal is getting through." He turned to the mike again and the sound of his voice echoed with a plaintive desperation in the silence of the room.

"Even if he'd blacked-out he would have recovered by now." The man who had suggested that perhaps the radio had broken whispered to his neighbour, a small technician with a twisted scar writhing across one cheek. "My guess is that Rosslyn couldn't take it."

"I doubt it." The scarred man shook his head. "They tested him remember. He stood ten gravities in the centrifuge."

"Yeah, but that ship hit twelve on the way up. It had to in order to reach the seven miles per second escape velocity before the fuel got too low. My guess is that…"

"Shut up," said Adams quietly. "If you can't keep lip buttoned get out."

"I only…"

"You heard me." Adams didn't raise his voice but the winced at the Colonel's tone, then, shrugging he fell silent.

"Curt! Comain calling. Curt! Answer me will you! Answer me!"

"How long now?" Adams rubbed his bloodshot eyes and Comain twisted in his seat as he looked at the Colonel.

"Three hours. He should have reported before this. He should have reported within the first ten minutes even if he did black-out. Something's wrong, Colonel. Curt wouldn't do if he could help it."

"No." Adams rubbed his eyes again. "Is the ship on course?"

"Tracking stations report that it took-off as per schedule. The observatories are reporting every fifteen minutes. As far as the ship itself is concerned everything is on the beam. If only Curt would answer." Comain bit his thin lips and leaned wards the radio again.

"Curt! Comain here. Come in, Curt! Make some sort of noise, damn you! Are you still alive?"

The radio hummed with a smooth surge of power and outside, high on a slender tower, the beam antenna focused on tiny point of the ship swung a little as it followed the course of the gleaming speck.

"He could be dead," said Adams sombrely. "The free radiation could have got him, or a meteor. Well," he shifted in his chair, "we can only hope that the automatics will bring the ship back again without him."

"He isn't dead," insisted Comain savagely. "He couldn't be dead. He…" He paused, his eyes behind their thick lenses widening as sound filtered from the humming radio.

"Comain… Curt here… Ill…. Answer."

"Curt!" The thin man's hands fluttered as he adjusted the dials, stepping up the beam power of the radio. "Speak up, man! Are you alright?"

"I…" The radio blurred to a sudden wash of static, then, with almost shocking abruptness, the thin voice steadied, seemed to gain power, as if the speaker stood in the very same room as the tensely listening men.

"Comain! Man it's good to hear your voice."

"What happened, Curt? Why didn't you answer sooner?"

"Acceleration twisted a wire, threw the radio out of kilter, that or the radiation up here altered the capacity of a coil. I could hear you, but you didn't seem to be hearing me."

"Right." Comain threw the switches of three recording machines. "Let's have it, Curt. You said that you were ill? Are you?"

"Yes." The pilot retched and the sound made the listening men glance uneasily at each other. "Nothing too serious—I hope. Free fall isn't a picnic, Comain. At first it wasn't too bad, probably the excitement kept me normal, but after a while I felt my stomach tie itself into knots and my last three meals are still floating around the cabin."

"Sickness." Comain made a rapid note. "Keep talking, Curt." He leaned over to the slumped figure of the Colonel. "Can we get the Doc here? Maybe he could suggest something to ease the sickness?"

"Get the doctor," ordered Adams and a man almost ran from the room to fetch the old medico. "Keep him talking, Comain. Is there anything else wrong with him?"

"I'm bleeding from nose and ears." The voice from the speaker faded then returned with roaring strength. "Blood cells ruptured during take-off. Normally it wouldn't matter but with this dope inside of me the blood isn't coagulating. Should I take the green injection?"

"We're getting the doctor. Better wait until he gets here before doing anything like that. How is the ship operating?"

"Vibration still a nuisance. I can feel the hull quivering and the stanchions haven't settled down yet."

"Vibration!" Comain glanced at Adams. "How? The rockets cut almost three hours ago."

"I know that." Curt retched again and when he spoke the listeners could imagine his inner pain. "I'm in a closed system remember. There's no air up here to damp out the vibration, and believe me, there was plenty to start with. It will damp out in time, but will it affect the instruments?"

"It shouldn't." Comain made a quick notation. "How is the radiation?"

"The Geiger's well into the red. Cosmic rays of course I'd guess at plenty of gamma particles as well." Curt paused. "I hope I don't go blind."

"You won't," said Comain with false conviction. He twisted in his seat as the old doctor entered the room, and gestured him towards the radio. "Curt's sick," he said rapidly. "Free fall doesn't agree with his stomach. He's bleeding, too."

"I'll talk to him." The doctor grunted as he settled his bulk into a chair. "Hello, Curt, I hear that you're having a trouble."

"Hello, Doc. Can you suggest anything to untwist my guts?"

"Sorry, Curt, but you'll just have to stand it. It's all in your mind you know. The balancing channels in the inner ear are out of kilter without a constant gravity drag to inform them which direction is 'down.' Your mind knows that you're falling, but your body knows that you are. You can't blame it too much, after all the body is only a reflex mechanism, it can only respond in a certain way to external stimuli. As soon as you can convince it that everything is alright you'll get rid of your sickness."

"Thanks, Doc," said Curt dryly. "You're a great help. What about this bleeding?"

"Nothing to worry about. You've broken some surface blood cells and will lose a little blood. It will stop in time, your blood still has some coagulating power, and you won't bleed to death, if that's what you're afraid of."

"Should I use the green injection?"

"No. For all we know the radiation up there may thicken your blood and if it were normal you'd die from clotting. Better leave well alone, Curt. After all, you didn't expect it to be a picnic did you?"

"Go to hell," said Curt, and the doctor shook his head as he heard the sounds of violent retching coming from the radio.

"Nothing we can do," he said to Comain. "If we sympathise with him it will make it worse. Rosslyn has courage, he doesn't need anyone to hold his hand. He'll get out of it on his own, or he won't get out of it at all. I'm sorry for him, but I'd still give my right arm to be where he is now."

"I know what you mean," said Comain, and from the assembled men came a murmur of agreement. They all envied the pilot. They all shared his troubles, his dangers, and all hoped to share his final success, and there wasn't one of them who wouldn't have cheerfully given up his hopes of heaven to have taken his place.

Adams rose tiredly from his chair.

"Nothing any of us can do now, except to wait," he said heavily. "Comain. You stand by the radio and try and keep Rosslyn talking into the recorders. The rest of you get out of here. I'm going to get some sleep and from the look of you, you'd better do the same. I'll send a relief, Comain. You look all in."

"I don't want a relief."

"Maybe not, but you're going to get one." Adams glared at the thin man. "Get some sense, man. The rocket has only just started, it won't be back for three days, and you're almost asleep now."

"I can stand it."

"You'll do as I order!"

"No, Adams." The thin man glared at the Colonel. "Curt is my friend and I'm going to stand by until he's safely back on Earth. Send a relief if you like, but I'm staying here!"

"Damn you, Comain!" Tiredness and irritation sharpened the Colonel's voice. "I'm in charge here and you'll do as I say!"

"No." Comain thinned his lips as he stared at the officer. "I don't come under your jurisdiction, Adams. I'm a civilian, not a soldier, and my first loyalty is to my friend."

"I…" Adams paused as the old doctor rested his hand on his arm. "What is it?"

"Why argue with him, Adams? Comain's doing no harm and he might do Rosslyn a lot of good. You can send over a radio relief, but why beat your head against a wall?"

"But the ship can't return for three days yet. You know the procedure, Doc. It will drive close to the Moon, be caught in the satellite's gravitational field and be swung in a circular orbit. At the exact moment the tubes will fire a short blast to break free from the Moon and drive the ship towards Earth. What can Comain do to help that? What sense is there in waiting by the radio for three days?"

"None," admitted the old doctor. "But let him do it, Adams."

"Very well." The Colonel shrugged and followed the rest of the men from the room. Comain stared after him for a moment, half-angry with himself for annoying the officer, and yet knowing that nothing would keep him from radio contact with his friend.

Inside the hut it began to grow warm with the heat of the rising sun. Outside, the barren desert shimmered beneath the solar furnace and the sky stretched from horizon to horizon, an inverted bowl of clear blue. Men moved listlessly about the area, tired after the rush preceding take-off, squinting up at the bowl of the sky as if they hoped to see the tiny speck of the rocket ship as it drove silently towards the Moon.

Comain saw nothing of that. He sat, his thin features tense and a little bitter with frustrated ambition, and listened to the voice of a man who spoke from where no other man had ever been.

"This is hell, Comain. It's like seasickness multiplied a thousand times. A horrible vertigo and nausea. We'll have to do something about it on future flights."

"We can rotate the ship, provide an artificial gravitation by means of centrifugal force. I'm more worried about the vibration you mentioned. Is it still bad?"

"Dying. Almost gone now."

"Good. What is it like out there, Curt?"

"Wonderful!" Despite the sickness Comain could catch the note of near-exultation in his friend's voice. "Space is black of course, we knew that, but the stars are like a million diamonds scattered on a piece of black velvet. I never guessed that there could be so many stars. We can't see them on Earth, the air is too thick, but out here they glow like electric lights. Fourth magnitude stars are brighter than first, and the really bright ones, Vega, Rigel, you know them as well as I do, they shine like headlights on a dark night."

"How are you feeling, Curt? In yourself I mean."

"My temperature has risen. Hundred and one point three. Pulse is ninety-five. I'm sweating, too, have been ever since take-off, and my skin itches a little."

"Badly?"

"No. Nervous reaction from take-off I suppose. I've noticed an ache in my bones and my muscles hurt a little. That could be the effect of free fall, I've had to learn to move all over again and may have strained a few tendons. One effect of this gravity lack is that my mind seems to be terribly clear. I can almost feel the blood rush through my skull and thoughts bubble and rise as yeast in fermenting wine. The things I've thought of, Comain! The ideas I've had. If I wasn't doubled up with vertigo this would be paradise, and even with the sickness I feel that I'm on top of the world."

"You are." Comain bit his lip as he recognised his own envy betraying itself in his tone, but the pilot didn't seem to notice. Curt yawned, the sound coming clearly over the radio, then gave an apologetic laugh.

"Funny. I feel tired. Think that I'll sleep for a while."

"Curt! Are you insane? You can't be tired, not with all that anti-fatigue drug they gave you before take-off. Are you alright, Curt?"

"Sure I'm alright. Just a little sleepy. I'll be as good as new after a while."

"Keep awake, Curt. Don't give in to it. Keep talking."

"I can't. I'm too tired…tired…tired…"

"Curt!" Hastily Comain adjusted the controls, feeding more power to the radio beam "Answer me, Curt! Curt!"

Silence. Nothing but the hum of the radio and the distant crackle of static, and after a long while the thin man admitted defeat. He pressed a button, waiting until a uniformed operator arrived to take over, then, his feet moving with an exaggerated slowness, walked tiredly from the room.

Above his bowed head the sun crawled across a sky of clearest blue and beneath his feet the sand plumed in little clouds as he walked wearily towards his quarters. Men passed him, stared curiously at his drawn features, and he passed then though they didn't exist.

When he finally fell asleep his dreams were filled with exotic worlds and strange races, or heroic men and heroic machines.

Slowly the day wore on.

CHAPTER IV

He awoke to the sound of shouts and sharp commands. A hand gripped his shoulder, shaking him and making the narrow cot on which he rested quiver and tremble.

"Comain! Wake up man. Wake up!"

"What?" He opened his eyes, blinking, trying to focus on the pale blob of a face which loomed above him. "What's the matter?"

"Hurry. Wake up."

He grunted, fumbling for his spectacles, hooking them behind his ears and blinking at the Colonel's worried expression. He felt ill, overtired, his head a mass of cotton wool and mouth tasting like the discharge end of a sewerage pipe. He gasped, feeling his clammy body shiver as the Colonel dragged off the sweat-soaked sheets, and he swung his thin legs over the edge of the bed as he struggled to regain full awareness.

"Adams! What's the matter?"

"Get up, Comain. We want you over at the radio. Quick!"

"Something wrong?" Panic seared through him and his hands trembled as he reached for his clothes. Adams nodded.

"Yes. Rosslyn has only just made radio contact after a silence of more than twelve hours and I'm worried."

"Twelve hours." Comain stared up at the Colonel. "As long as that?"

"Yes."

"Why didn't you call me sooner?"

"Why should I?" Adams moved his shoulders beneath the thin material of his tunic. "What good would it have done? You were tired, we all were, and a man was standing by the radio all the time. You needed sleep, and you've had it, twelve hours of it."

"Yes." Comain finished dressing and licked his dry lips. He stepped over to the small water faucet and laved his face and hands, then, after letting the tepid water run for a moment, drank three glasses of the warm fluid. "What's wrong?"

"I'll tell you on the way over." Adams shifted his feet with nervous impatience. "Ready yet?"

"Ready."

Together they stepped from the hut into the soft darkness of approaching night.

"The ship isn't keeping to schedule," said Adams quietly. "The observatories report that it is going too fast, that, even though it will pass through the gravitational field of the Moon, it will only be swung from a direct flight line, and not swung into a circular orbit." He paused and in the silence Comain could hear the sound of their boots as they scuffed over the sand.

"Impossible."

"Don't be a fool, Comain. It's happening, I tell you. The observatories can't be wrong."

"But how could it happen? We know exactly, know to the third decimal place, just what thrust we get from the fuel, the duration of fire from the venturis, the speed of the ship, everything. It started as predicted. It should continue like that."

"It isn't." Adams stared at the thin man. "Something's gone wrong with the automatics, Comain. That is obvious. Now, unless Rosslyn can operate the ship by manual control, he will drive directly into space."

"Yes," said the thin man numbly. "I know that."

He didn't say any more. Neither did the Colonel. Each was thinking of the same thing, but, true to their natures, each placed a different priority on what they were thinking.

Adams thought of a ship driving into space, carrying with it a helpless man. Comain thought of a man, his friend, being carried into the unknown by rebel machinery. He was glad when they finally entered the crowded radio shack.

"Anything?" He thrust the radio operator from his seat as the man shook his head, then, with fingers which trembled a little, he adjusted the power flow of the beam radio.

"Curt! Comain here. Answer please."

"Comain!" The thin man flushed to the welcome in the voice of a man almost a quarter million miles away. "Been asleep?"

"Yes. When you decided to take a rest I followed your example." He frowned a question at the Colonel, and Adams shook his head. "Keep talking, Curt. I'll be with you in a moment."

"Why? Is anything wrong down there?"

"Of course not, Curt. Just give any relevant data you can think of. I want to check the radio directional antenna." He signalled to the operator and stepped over to Adams. "Doesn't he know?"

"Not yet. I didn't want to tell him until we knew just what to do. In any case, he's only just made contact, I can't understand why he should have fallen asleep."

"The radiation perhaps?" Comain shrugged. "Not that it matters now. The main thing is to get the rocket back on course. Have you the observatory reports?"

"Yes. The ship will reach the orbit of the Moon within an hour. The gravitational field will swing it and it will be hidden from sight for about two hours. After that...."

"If he can't operate the manual controls he will just drive on a straight line into space." Comain nodded, his thin features grim. "So what must be done must be done quickly."

"Yes. Once the ship is hidden by the Moon there'll be radio no contact, and after that, with the speed the ship has, we can't count on more than a few minutes. Hurry, Comain! Hurry!"

"Yes." Comain returned to the radio and leaned towards the microphone. "Curt. Can you receive me?"

"Yes."

"Good. Now listen, Curt. Listen carefully. Something has gone wrong with the ship. You are travelling too fast. You must take over the operation of the ship. Do you understand me?"

"I understand."

"Good. Now this is what you must do. Spin the main gyroscope until you have reversed positions in space, until the firing tubes are pointed in your direction of flight. When you have done that fire the main drive for exactly ten seconds. No more. Understand?"

"Yes." Curt laughed and something of the tension in the room left the waiting men. "Don't sound so serious, Comain. This is why I'm here isn't it? Despite what you say your machines could never replace a man. They break down and when they do they are helpless. Relax, Comain. I'll bring your ship back to you."

"You have an hour, Curt. One hour in which to slow down the speed of the ship and bring it back to the scheduled flight path. After that time you will be hidden behind the Moon and I won't be able to talk to you. Also, and this is important, the ship doesn't have enough fuel to return without the aid of the Moon's gravitational field to swing and slow the vessel. Work fast, Curt. Work fast."

"I'm working," said the pilot grimly. "Hear me?"

Over the radio came the whine of the gyroscopes as they spun on their bearings, turning the ship on its short axis, shifting the vessel in direct ratio to their own mass. It was a thing which took time. The mass of the gyroscope was only one hundred thousandth of that of the entire ship and it would take exactly one hundred thousand revolutions to turn the vessel. During that time they could do nothing but wait.

And wait they did.

They waited while the slender hand of a chronometer crawled towards the deadline. They sweated blood as, a quarter of a million miles away, a man fought for his life. It took more than thirty minutes for the spinning gyroscope to rotate the ship, thirty minutes of heart-numbing waiting before the gaping venturis were in a position to check the speed of the ship. And then…

The rockets wouldn't fire!

Comain winced as he heard Curt's startled curse.

"The tubes! They won't respond. Comain!"

"Steady." The thin man bit his lip as he stared at the swinging hand of the chronometer. "The take-off may have jarred loose a wire. Check the contacts."

More waiting. Sitting and standing in a mounting tension while over the radio came the gasping breath of a man working in impossible conditions to effect an emergency repair.

Contact checked but it's still no damn use."

"Wait!" Comain glanced at Adams. "Curt. There is only one thing you can do now. Lift the hatch and press the firing relay by hand. Can you do that?"

"I can try," said the pilot grimly. "Won't the automatics take over at the correct time?"

"Yes, but, Curt, that will be too late. You've only got fifteen minutes left before you slip behind the Moon. The automatics are set for time, not distance, and they won't fire for several hours yet. Your only chance is to fire the rockets manually—and you must do it within the next thirty minutes."

"I understand. I'm working on the hatch now."

Over the radio came the sound of a man's laboured breathing and the faint ringing of metal on metal. In imagination Comain followed the pilot's movements. First the thin metal hatch sealing the control room. It was fastened with catches and shouldn't take long to remove. A clanging sound and he knew that it had been thrown aside, then, mingling with the sound of his harsh breathing, Curt's voice echoed from the speaker.

"Damn gloves! Can't grip anything. Take them off. That's better. Now. This conduit to the firing relays. Which wires? Which wires?"

"The red ones," snapped Comain. "Can you hear me, Curt? Trace the red ones."

"Got 'em. Now." A mumbling and then a savage curse. "Damn free fall! Damn it to hell! Damn all designers who can't imagine a man having to repair a machine. How the hell can I get down there?"

"Curt!" Comain bit his lips until the blood ran over his chin. "What's the matter now?"

"The hatch is too narrow." Curt's voice echoed through the room. "I can't get down far enough to reach the relay."

"Your G-suit. Take it off."

"Yes. That's an idea. Funny I never thought of that." Comain glanced at Adams as the pilot's voice vibrated from the speaker. He thinned his lips at the sound of the pilot's voice, his eyes narrowing in sudden suspicion, then, before he could speak, Curt spoke again.

"There. Suit's off. Now let me see." The sound of violent retching interrupted the too-calm tones of the pilot. "Damn it! Now to work. Hook one foot behind the chair. Grip the edge of the hatch. Thrust downwards, stretch..." His voice grew muffled and over the radio came the sound of gasping and scraping. Comain glanced at the chronometer, his pale face wet with the sweat of nervous tension.

"Hurry, Curt. Hurry!"

"Got it." Comain sighed with relief at the triumph in the pilot's voice. Now, press this and..."

Nothing happened. No thunder spilled from the radio. No pulse of blasting rocket tubes as they checked the speed of the distant rocket ship. Just silence and the rasping breath of a desperate man.

"Curt. Nothing happened. What's wrong now?"

"What's wrong?" Comain hardly recognised the voice of his friend. "You smug fools! You knew didn't you! You trusted metal before flesh and blood. Damn you, Comain! Damn you to hell!"

"Curt! Take it easy, man. What's the matter?"

"The relay's broken, that's what. The metal snapped in my hand like a piece of glass."

"What?" Comain stared at Adams, then, even as the Colonel stared the question, he knew what must have happened. The vibration of the ship had altered the structure of the metal of the relay. It had crystallised, changed from strength to weakness, shaken and tormented by vibration and radiation. It was a chance in a million, the one thing they hadn't even thought of guarding against, but it had happened and now...

"Curt." Comain wiped sweat from his streaming forehead. "You'll have to by-pass the relay. Get lower down into the hatch and connect the wires by hand. Can you do it, Curt? Curt. Answer me."

"I hear you, Comain. I'll try and do what you say, but my head feels funny, I can't seem to make my hands obey me. Connect the green wires you say?"

"The red ones, Curt. The red ones."

"Right, Comain. I'll try it. Connect the red wires. Connect."

Silence replaced the steady sounds from the radio. A deep silence, divorced from any trace of noise but the steady hiss of the carrier beam.

Comain lunged for the controls, adjusting the power flow and altering the settings with delicate touches of his slender fingers, but, even as he did so he knew that what he did was wasted time.

The ship had passed behind the Moon.

CHAPTER V

Two hours the observatories had said. Two hours before the ship, if it did not alter course, could be seen again. There would be a short while before radio contact was broken, before the ship had speeded beyond the point where its signal could be picked up and amplified, and after that...

Comain didn't like to think about it.

He sat before the radio, conscious of the eyes of the waiting men as they stared at him, and for the thousandth time he cursed himself for forgetting the unsuspected. Adams sat beside him and the naked glare of the electric fights shone on his grizzled hair, accentuating the deep lines running from nose to mouth, making him seem suddenly old and feeble.

"How soon will we know?"

"If Curt can fire the rockets we should know within an hour. If not..." Comain shrugged.

"Can he get to the controls?"

"I don't know. There was no reason why he should. Who could have thought that the ship would travel so fast? Or that the vibration would crystallise just that piece of metal?"

"Can he get to the firing point?" Adams repeated doggedly. He didn't seem capable of thinking of anything else.

"I don't know," snapped Comain irritably. "He may be able to. I just don't know."

"Think of it," whispered a man. "He's up there, sick, burning with radiation fever, trying to fix the firing controls and save his life. I've worked on those relays and I say that he can't do it. Not in the time and without the proper tools he can't."

"Shut up." Adams glared at the man. "If you must talk, talk outside."

"What the hell?" The man glared at the Colonel. "This is a free country isn't it? Can't a man speak his mind now?"

"So you don't think that he can reach the firing point?" Comain stared at the man. "Why not?"

"Because it was never designed to be reached from the control room, that's why. I've worked on it, and I never did like the idea of trusting to automatics so much. If that relay has broken it means that he's got to strip off half the wiring and then, even if he can do that, he's got to squeeze down the hatch and connect the wires direct. You know what that means."

"You think that the acceleration pressure will be too much for him?"

The man shrugged, reaching in his pocket for a cigarette. "You designed the ship," he reminded. "What do you think?"

Comain nodded, feeling a growing sickness at the pit of his stomach. The man was right. He had designed the ship, and, perhaps subconsciously, he had tended to ignore the human element. He had trusted too much in machines, in things of metal and plastic, of wire and crystal. He had toyed with a wholly automatic vessel with the pilot a passenger rather than the main element which he should have been.

And he could have been the cause of his friend's death.

But there was still hope. Curt could fire the rockets by hand. He could check the speed of the ship, fall into the gravitational field of the Moon; restore the vessel to its pre-determined path. It would take so little. Just the contact of two red wires. Such a little thing, and yet, knowing what he knew, Comain shivered to a sudden doubt.

He didn't like dealing with the human element. Machines were predictable. The field of cybernetics offered so much and he had only agreed to work on the ship because of Curt and because of his youthful dreams. Now he was finished, this he would leave the field of rocketry and concentrate on cybernetics. He...

"One hour gone," said Adams grimly, and seemed to slump even further into his chair.

"He can't make it." The man who had spoken before glared around the room. "Rosslyn's as good as dead. He doesn't stand a chance, and we know it."

"I've told you once," said Adams quietly. "Do I have to tell you again?"

"It could have been me." The man ignored the unspoken threat in the Colonel's tone. "It could have been any of us. Damn it all I don't mind taking a chance, no man does, but to be trapped up there without a ghost of a chance of getting just because of faulty design..." He glared at Comain. "To me that's just like murder."

"It couldn't be helped. Do you think we did it deliberately?" Adams stared at the man and his grizzled hair and seamed gave him a peculiarly brutal expression. "Damn you! To hear you talk you'd think that we deliberately sent Rosslyn up there knowing that he could never get back."

"You could have used a little more brain. Didn't it ever occur to you that something might go wrong? What's the good of sending a man in a ship like that if he can't get at anything?"

"You..." Adams surged from his chair, his eyes twin flecks of feral rage. "You and your big mouth. I'll..."

"Steady, Adams." Comain grabbed the Colonel by the arm and thrust him back into his chair. "Take it easy, the man is right."

"What?"

"He's right in what he says. We should have been able to predict what happened. A machine could do it, but we aren't machines. How could we guess that the vibration at take-off would crystallise the relay? We just didn't accept that as a factor at all, but if we'd had a large enough calculator, a machine capable of considering every potential thing which could happen, we'd have known."

"I don't understand." Adams frowned at the thin man. "What are you talking about, Comain?"

"You've heard of EINAC I suppose? You know that there are huge electronic machines which are able to store a series of facts and to predict, within the range of those facts, a probable happening? Insurance companies do it all the time. They can tell almost exactly just how many people will die from any large group. They can even give the average life expectancy of any trade or profession. You know that don't you?"

"Yes," admitted Adams reluctantly. "But what has that to do with what's happening now?"

"If we'd had such a machine, one large enough to store all the relevant factors, we could have told to within a fraction of a decimal point just what chances Curt would have of survival. We could have adjusted the variables to give him the highest possible favourable probability factor and we'd have known in advance just what would happen. As it was we merely took a wild gamble. We didn't know what would happen once the ship took off. We guessed, but we guessed wrong, and now a man may lose his life because of it."

"So what do you suggest? That we don't build any more space ships until this dream-machine of yours has been built?" Adams smiled without humour and Comain knew that the Colonel thought that he was just talking to ease his inner tension. In a way Adams was right. Comain admitted it, but, as he watched the swinging hands of the chronometer, he knew that it was more than just that.

He really believed in such a machine. Like most weak people he had a fear of the unknown. He had always disliked meeting new people, of making sudden decisions, of thrusting himself forward. It would be so simple if there were such a machine as he had described. Then, whenever a new problem arose, the exact percentage of probability could be found and acted on. There would be no wasted time, the result of an experiment could be found without the experiment actually taking place. The machine would know everything there was to be known. It would have all the knowledge of the ages within its memory banks, would be able to scan that knowledge, and, from that information, deduct new facts and predict inevitable happenings.

It would be an oracle. An omnipotent, omnipresent, machine. It would end all fear. It would end all blind alleys and futile lines of research. It would free men forever from the necessity of studying all their lives so that, with luck, they could add just one new fact before their deaths.

A grunt from one of the men snapped him from his dream back to the present.

"Five minutes before the ship comes into sight again."

"Get the radio antenna aligned on the point of emergence," snapped Adams. "We won't have long before he's beyond range."

Comain nodded and fed co-ordinates from the observatory into the machine before him. On its high tower the hug web of the radio antenna swung a little as it pointed toward glowing face of the Moon.

Tensely they waited for the radio to crackle into life, and in silence, the steady hiss of the carrier beam seemed to mock them with its indifferent noise.

Three minutes. Comain wiped sweat from his face and neck, wondering desperately what he was going to say.

Two minutes. He checked the three recording machines, and made a slight adjustment to the controls of the radio.

One minute. Comain switched on the recorders and made sure that his headset was near at hand.

Now. Everyone stared at the black box of the radio speaker and Comain leaned forward, clearing his throat with a rasping sound.

"Curt! Comain here. Can you receive me?"

Silence and the steady hiss of the carrier wave.

"Curt! Come in, Curt. Answer. Answer."

A crackle. A blur of static and, like a thin ghost, the weak voice of a man at the extreme range of radio reception.

"Comain. Thank God you waited."

"Did you fix it?" He knew that it was a foolish thing to ask but for the moment he couldn't think of anything else to say. The radio hummed and faded, crackled and blurred. Impatiently Comain fed power into the extra boosters and the voice returned with a rush.

"Fix it?" The laugh which followed wasn't nice to hear. "I fixed it alright. If I'd had a bomb I'd have fixed it for good. You and your damn machines."

"What happened? Curt! What happened?"

"I couldn't reach it, that's what happened. I tried to get down to the firing controls. I could see them just beyond my fingers, but I couldn't get down far enough. Can you understand that, Comain? I could actually see them." Static washed through the speaker and the men moved a little closer, hungry to catch the last words of the man in space.

"I stripped off the G-suit. I stripped off the undersuit. I still couldn't get down far enough. I grew desperate then. It's funny how a man will grow desperate when he still thinks there's a chance. I cut a vein and covered my body with my own blood. I thought that it would let me slip those last few inches, a sort of oil you know, but it didn't work. I couldn't do it, Comain. A half-inch difference in the width of the hatch would have done it. Three inches difference in the position of the firing point would have done it. Even a single tool would have enabled me to fire the drive, but I didn't have it, Comain. I didn't have it."

"Couldn't he have used his feet?" A man whispered the suggestion, then fell silent as the radio blurred again.

"Have you ever tried stripping wire and connecting them with your toes, Comain? I did. I ripped the nails from both feet trying, but it was no good. You chose your wiring well. It would take a knife to get through the insulation and I hadn't got a knife. I hadn't got anything except my teeth." Curt laughed again. "I can taste my own blood now."

"God!" A man stumbled towards the door, his face white and his eyes sick and dark against his strained features. Adams stared after him then stepped towards the radio.

"Rosslyn. How are your physical symptoms?"

"I'm scared, Colonel. As scared as all hell. I'm going to die. You know that don't you? I know it, and so you know it, too."

"Never mind that now. How are your physical symptoms? Has the radiation affected you at all?"

"Radiation?" Curt sounded puzzled. "What are you talking about?"

"Snap out of it man." Adams glared at the radio. You know what I mean. Has the radiation affected you at all?"

"I don't know. How could I know? I've been busy trying to fix up this glorified firework. Damn you and your questions anyway. Why the hell should I answer?"

"Curt." Comain thrust Adams away from the radio. "Don't be bitter about it. We couldn't help it, you know that. You took a chance and you lost, but, if you had the chance again, would you refuse?"

"Thanks, Comain, I knew that you'd understand." The faint voice echoed with a peculiar gratefulness from the speaker. "Would I take it again? I don't know. It hasn't been pleasant up here. All on my own, doubled with sickness, knowing that I'm going to die. I don't want to die, Comain. I want to enjoy all the things I haven't had time to enjoy. I want to smell the scent of growing things, to feel the rain on my face, and to see the sunset and the night sky. I want to marry, have some kids perhaps; grow to be an old man. I shan't have any of those things now, Comain. I shall never know what they are like, the things I haven't had. All I've got now is a tank of air, a tank of water, and the universe to rove in. It's a big universe Comain, but I don't think that I shall be seeing much of it."

"Curt." Comain bit his lips until the blood ran down his chin. "Curt—I'm sorry."

"Sorry? Why, Comain. Because I am going to die instead of you? Don't feel sorry for me. Just see that they spell my name right in the history books. One other thing. Tell Adam not to worry too much about the radiation. I don't feel any effects from it."

Static crackled from the radio and the thin, ghost voice, wavered and blurred, fading and dwindling to a tiny thread of sound.

"Goodbye, Comain. I don't regret this you know, but if only that hatch had been wider, a half-inch even." Comain frowned as he listened to the dying voice. "Remember my name, won't you. I'd like to think that I won't be wholly forgotten. You know how to spell it? Rosslyn. R…O…S…S…"

Sound snarled from the speaker. A savage burst of noise, thundering, pulsing, and then, as if it had been stopped at source, silence replaced the noise, silence and the empty hiss of the carrier beam.

"The automatics," whispered Comain sickly. "They fired on time."

"Then he's safe?" Adams stared at the thin man and sweat glistened on his seamed features. Comain shook his head.

"No. The blast came too late. Anyway, the stress must have split the hull. If the metal of the relay had crystallised then other metal must have been weakened also. Not that it makes any difference now."

"Then he's dead?"

"Perhaps. What difference does it make? If the hull didn't split and release his air, killing him instantly, then he will still die. He's locked in a wrecked ship with little air, little water; no food. We didn't think that he'd need food on a three-day trip. Whatever happens, dead or not, we'll never see him again."

"I see." Adams gulped, then, the training of a lifetime asserting itself, straightened his back and strode towards the door. "We must assume that he died in the blast. The radio wouldn't have cut out the way it did if the control cabin had remained intact. I must report this. Will he fall into the Sun?"

"I doubt it. With its present speed and course the ship will continue into outer space. It may hit an asteroid, be thrown off course by impact with a meteor, or it may be drawn into the gravitational field of some planet. We don't know yet, but it doesn't matter now, does it? Curt is dead. My friend is dead—and I helped to kill him."

He left the room then, walking on unfeeling feet, his thin features twisted with inner anguish, his weak eyes staring blankly before him. Outside the stuffy room the Moon cast a soft radiance over the firing area, and he stared at it, hating its once-friendly face.

Curt was dead.

He sat, a stiffened corpse in the wreck of a ship which been his dream, and his empty eyes stared at the cold glory of the glittering stars. They were cruel those stars. They kindled dreams in the hearts of men and they snatched those dreams away. Once, a long time ago now it seemed, two boys had stared at those stars and had dreamed of blazing a trail of fantastic adventure between the spinning orbs of alien worlds. Boyish dreams, but to them they had been very real. Curt and Comain. Together in incredible adventure, and now…

Curt was dead.

He bumped into a man, not seeing him, not seeing anything and, stumbling a little, continued on his way into the night. The man stared after him, frowning, half-decided to follow the tall, thin person with the deathly white face. He shrugged, feeling a little troubled, a little uneasy, and, at the same time, a little disgusted. It was not often that a grown man walked the desert crying like a child.

CHAPTER VI

The man had a thick neck, thick wrists, thick body, and eyebrows so thick that they looked like a bar of black metal resting above his eyes. His clothes hugged the body of a prize fighter but his voice, when he spoke, was the voice of an educated man.

"Mr. Comain?"

"Yes?" Comain hesitated on the porch of the small house he rented, key in his hand, and looked at his visitor. The man smiled.

"Shall we go inside?" There was no accent and his tones were cultured and yet Comain knew that the man was not speaking his native tongue. There was a certain preciseness, an unnatural perfection only to be acquired by an adult learning a foreign language and being satisfied with nothing but perfection. That very perfection, the way he spoke, betrayed the very thing which he had striven to hide. Comain shrugged and opened the door.

Inside, the house was a mess. Comain lived alone and lived only for his work. Heavy technical books cluttered the tables, filled the chairs, spilled on to the faded carpet on the floor and rested like multi-coloured boxes, on rows of sagging chairs. Parts of semi-dismantled apparatus lay on a bench and a sheet of black insulation was studded with the blank faces of registering dials.

The stranger looked around, cleared some of the books from a chair, dusted the seat, and sitting down, took a cigarette from a gold-chased, silver case. He offered it to the lean man and Comain shook his head.

"No thank you." He dragged a stool from beneath the table and sat down, resting his elbows on the scarred wood. "What can I do for you?"

"For me?" The man smiled. "Perhaps it is I who can do something for you." He hesitated. "Permit me to introduce myself, my name is Smith, John Smith." He frowned at Comain's involuntary smile. "I amuse you?"

"Your lack of imagination does."

"How so?"

"Your choice of name is hardly one to arouse confidence. American?"

"No."

"English?"

"Does that matter?"

"It could," said Comain deliberately. "Even though I am no longer working for the government yet I still come beneath Security regulations.

Either you are very naive or you take me for a fool." He rose and headed towards the door. "I think that you had better go now." The stranger didn't move.

"You move too fast," he murmured, "and in the wrong direction. I have no intention of asking you to betray your trust."

"No?"

"No." Smoke plumed from the slim cigarette. "Please sit down, there is much we need to discuss." He waited until Comain, moving with a slow reluctance, resumed his position on the stool. "You see," said Smith casually, "the people whom I represent know quite a bit about you. They know that you were employed on rocketry and that you left the field five years ago. They also know that you are probably the most advanced expert in the field of cybernetics and electronic computers. They are not interested in anything but that." He flipped ash from his cigarette. "I am here to offer you employment in that field."

"I see." Comain stared at the littered room. "Is this a clumsy attempt to bribe me? I may be a scientist and I know that the popular conception of all scientists is that they are misguided idealists without any awareness of what goes on outside their circle, but I am not wholly a fool. Admitted I no longer work for the government, in fact I work for no one but myself, but that doesn't mean I'm willing to turn traitor to any foreign power offering me a job."

"Did I mention the word 'traitor'?" Smith shook his head. "Believe me when I say that is the last thing required of you. No. I am simply here to make you an offer, an offer which, as a gentleman, you are at perfect liberty to refuse without ill-feeling." He shrugged. "It is not so long ago that such offers from one nation to a citizen of another were common. Now, owing to the fanatical regulations, it is not so common."

"It is a crime to accept," snapped Comain. "I shouldn't even listen to you, you know that."

"Why not?" Smith gestured with his cigarette. "Please let us not be stupid about this. After all, what am I doing? I am making you an offer, is that a crime? I am talking to you, is that wrong? Would it be wrong for you to listen to me? Can you deny the existence of a fact, negate it, by refusing to admit its place in the scheme of things? Really, Comain, as a scientist you should know better."

"Your logic does not impress me," said Comain coldly. He stared at his visitor. "I will admit that no harm can come by my listening to what you have to say, but I must warn you, I will not promise to respect your confidence. I am still a citizen and this is still my country."

"A patriot?" Smith stared curiously at the scientist. "After all that has been done to you?"

"So I lost my job and they kicked me out of the research laboratories. So what?" Comain didn't try to hide his bitterness. "They didn't like it when I refused to follow their orders, work along the same old useless lines, and when I tried to show them where they were wrong they fired me."

"Misuse of equipment," murmured Smith. "Insubordination and an incorrect attitude towards the problem as a whole." He shrugged. "The commercial field perhaps, or no, they are even more stringent."

"I was blacklisted." Comain wiped his thick lenses. "General Electric. Du Ponts. Amalgamated Power. They all turned me down." He laughed with brittle anger. "Make one wrong step in this set-up and you're out on your ear—for good!"

"I see." Smith looked down at the glowing tip of his cigarette. "So you work at home." He glanced at the equipment, his heavy features expressionless. "Have you had success?"

"How could I?" Comain's shoulders sagged with the weight of bitterness. "Look at the stuff. Junk! Rubbish from the surplus stores. Discarded because it was no good. How can I build a delicate mechanism from that?"

"But your theories, they have progressed?"

"A little." Enthusiasm warmed the bleak voice as Comain spoke of his dream. "You know what I'm after, of course?"

"A thinking machine, is it not? A robot?" Smith waved his cigarette. "I am not a scientist, remember, but I have a grasp of the general pattern."

"A thinking machine." Comain shrugged. "Say it like that and it's easy. A robot. Say it that way and it's easier still."

"But there are thinking machines. The big electronic computers, the initial machines?" Smith paused and held out the butt of his cigarette. Comain took it from him and crushed it out on the floor.

"You are suffering from the same delusion most people suffer from. You mention the MANIAC, the EINAC, and other initial machines. You talk of electronic computers, and all you really talking about are glorified adding machines. They do not think. They perform routine operations, perform them at incredible speeds, but that is all. There isn't a single machine in existence which can be truly called a 'thinking machine', In fact, the general trend among the operators of such machines is to restrict what they mean by the term 'thinking' as something the machines cannot do."

"But…" Smith looked bewildered. "I understood…" Comain shrugged.

"You understood that I am working on the problem of thinking machines, and so I am." He leaned a little further across the littered table. "Let us look at the problem and see what it is we're up against. First, it isn't enough just to construct a machine which will hold information. We already have such machines, we call them libraries. It isn't enough to build a collection of glass and wire which can add faster, or compute faster than the human brain. We have that sort too, from the adding machines in offices to the big, initial machines at Washington. They are merely work horses. They can do nothing but what they are designed to do, and only routine mathematical work at that. They are no more thinking machines than a selenium switch which turns on the light when it grows dark can be called a thinking machine. The principle is the same in both cases, relays operated by external stimuli. A true thinking machine needs something more than that."

"I follow you," murmured Smith and his big body settled more comfortably in the chair. Comain shrugged.

"I'm telling you nothing which you could not learn from outside sources. The problem is well known, opinion only differs as to how it should be solved."

"Of course, and your solution?"

"I haven't got one—not yet." The lean man stared at the litter of dismantled equipment lying all over the ground of the small house. "To find the answer it is essential to go back to the basics. What is thought? What is that subtle something which makes a man different from all other animals? His brain is the same, structurally the same at least, and his body functions just like that of any animal. He is an animal but—he can think. When we discover just how and why then we will be able to build true thinking machines."

"I don't quite follow." Smith frowned, the thick eyebrows writhing over his forehead. "Surely if a sufficiently complicated machine were built, incorporating the sum total of human knowledge, we would have the answer?"

"Would we?" Comain almost sneered. "You think so? Answer this then. How would you define the word 'food'?"

"As something to eat."

"So. Is wood food? Termites eat wood and so it must be classified beneath that title. Is iron food? Rust corrodes, 'eats' iron. Is salt? Sodium chloride is made of two poisons and would it be logical to assume that two poisons can be eaten with safety?" Comain smiled at his visitor's expression. "You see, we, human beings, that is, have a very efficient and compact system of idea association. When we think of 'food' we may think of a steak, or an egg, or a stick of celery. It doesn't matter because we know that food isn't just the thing we think of. That only serves as a memory-identification to bring all our knowledge of what food is, what it does, how it tastes, all the knowledge we have ever learned about food, to the forefront of our consciousness. A machine can't think like that. Every item has to be fed in separately. Food to a machine is a steak or an egg, or a stick of celery. Not and/or either. That is only one word, remember, one concept. When you think of the thousands of words, the concepts, the ideas which the average brain handles during the course of a single day, then you will perhaps realise just what we're up against."

"So the problem is insoluble then?"

"I didn't say that." Comain rose and began pacing the room, pausing now and then to touch or examine some piece of equipment. "Perhaps we shall never be able to build a replica of a human brain. We don't want to. There would be no point in doing it when there are so many efficient units already in existence." He smiled at Smith's expression. "I refer to men, of course, there are millions of them, each with a highly efficient brain. No. What we must do is to build something better than we already have. A machine, able to think, able to absorb knowledge, to use that knowledge to increase its data, and to apply that knowledge in the best possible way."

"I begin to see what you are driving at," said the big man slowly. "A machine, of course, would not die. Therefore it would be possible to add tremendously to its store of data and if it could correlate that information…" He looked a thin man. "Deus Machina?"

"In a way, but it is up to men to prevent the machine ever becoming a God." Comain returned to the table and sat down. "You are right when you talk of potential immortality for the machine. There is no reason why it should not last a million years, and at that time it could be absorbing knowledge, finding new facts, solving all those problems which we simply haven't time to solve. The way things are now a scientist can't learn fast enough to have any time left for research. Aside from that the fields are becoming too specialised. A worker in biology, say, can't spare the time to learn about radioactives, and yet the field of radiant energy probably holds the answer to cellular breakdown, cancer, anaemia, and virulent disease. A metallurgist knows little about bacteria, and yet it has been shown that bacteria, certain strains that is, have an effect on metal. Time is the answer, Smith. Time. And we just haven't got enough of it."

He waved away the stranger's offer of a cigarette and sat, fuming with inward pain as he stared at the litter of junk around him. Time. Five years ago he had listened to his one friend die in the loneliness of space and within him the loss was a constant, unhealing wound. Trouble had followed, inevitably as, driven by a complex emotion stemming from both the subconscious death wish born of self-guilt and the desire to join Rosslyn, and the attitude of authority which, after the fatal flight, had abandoned true rocketry for the establishment of space stations, he had kicked over the traces.

There had been that time when he had wasted a month's research by unauthorised investigation into the reactions of metal-eating bacteria on the heavy metals. There had been the fight with a laboratory assistant, a fight which had left him weak and ill from both physical punishment and frustrated hate. The word had passed to the psychologists, then to Security, and he was dismissed from all access to vital information as an unstable risk. The rest had followed automatically.

The succession of commercial jobs, each worse than the last, ending finally in court proceedings for the theft of five grammes of platinum wire. He had got off with a fine and a warning—and Security lived on his neck for the next two years.

Now?

He stared at the junk, the salvaged pieces from surplus stores, the crude, too crude equipment and resisters. Scaled-down voltmeters when he needed to measure micro-volts. Hand-made radiation counters when he needed encephalographs. Steel-chassis when he needed non-magnetic conductors. The futility of what he was trying to do made him feel sick.

"It is hard, is it not?" Smith gestured with his cigarette and Comain realised that the thick man had followed his thoughts. "Genius should not be hampered by petty worries and the spite of little men. When you have built your predictor…"

"Predictor?" Comain stared at the big man and his eyes narrowed a little behind their thick lenses. "Who said anything about that?"

"But your machine will include prediction, will it not?"

"Maybe." Comain nervously ran his tongue over his dry lips. "I'm beginning to get it now," he said thoughtfully. "You aren't interested in the full potentials of a thinking machine. All you want is a predictor, and I can guess why."

"Indeed?"

"You want it for war. You want to use it to blast humanity to dust. You want it to gain an edge over the other nations."

"Perhaps." The big man smiled through the smoke of his cigarette. "Did the first man to discover fire intend his discovery to be used for incendiary bombs? Of course he didn't. And neither do we want to use your machine for war but, if it can be so used…" He shrugged. "This is a hard world, my friend, and we must be realists. Your friend died in space but did he risk his life so that the Moon could be used as a military base, or did he risk, and lose it, so that the old dream of interplanetary flight could be advanced? We cannot dictate how our discoveries are to be used, Comain, but does that mean no new discoveries should be made? And there is a proverb, I think. Half a loaf is better than none. To build your machine, no matter for what ostensible purpose, is better than not to build it at all. But—it will be a predictor, will it not?"

"It will."

"Are you certain of that? Our reports…" He smiled. "You understand how these things are. Fear has crushed the free exchange of scientific knowledge so that it is difficult to be certain about many matters."

"The machine, if and when built, will be the finest predictor in existence." Comain didn't look at his visitor. "Aside from the thinking ability all that is necessary to make a fairly accurate prediction is plenty of data, the more the better. If the weather stations had access to hidden reports as to cloud and wind, temperature and humidity, their reports would double in accuracy. The same with a machine. Feed it with everything known about the problem, let it correlate that information, assess variables and allow for errors, and you will have a modern oracle."

"Are you certain of that?"

"Yes."

"I see." Smith drew deeply on his cigarette, the tip glowing like a red eye against the impassiveness of his features. "Will you build one for us?"

"No."

Smith didn't seem surprised. He merely sat, inhaling the blue smoke from his cigarette, but his eyes held a hidden purpose. Comain fidgetted on his stool.

"I guessed that this was coming and I warned you. I will not betray my country."

"Have I asked you to?"

"No, but…"

"I, we, offer you full facilities to build your machine. I am not asking you to leave your employment. I am not even asking you to work for us instead of your own country. You are not working, your country neither needs your machine or will give you the opportunity to build it. How then will you be a traitor if you work for us?"

"Logic," said Comain bitterly. "It can prove anything."

"Let me be frank with you." Smith leaned a little further across the littered table. "We need you and what you could build. Those I represent have all the material wealth they can use but with that wealth they have a tremendous population and supply problem. The old methods are breaking down. It isn't enough to have an army of clerks and floors of computing machines. There are questions they cannot answer and questions that must be answered. How much grain to plant to take care of the increase in population? Where to build a dam to give the maximum amount of irrigation and power? How many tons of iron to be mined for how many planes? Where should development be speeded and why? What animals to breed and how many? Questions, Comain, which affect the life of a nation and, indirectly, the welfare of the world." He crushed the butt of his cigarette into smouldering ruin. "You understand me?"

"How many planes to carry how many bombs?" Comain didn't try to hide his cynicism. "When to fire the atomic missile and where? What weight of explosive to crush an enemy? When to attack to gain the greatest chance of success? Yes. Such a predictor could answer your questions, but it could answer others, too."

"Is fire to be banned because it can burn?" Smith shrugged. "I am not asking you to work for war but for peace. A hungry nation is a restless one—and soon the people will be hungry."

"A threat, Smith?"

"No, Comain. A prediction."

"I see." The lean man sighed and again his eyes drifted over the junk littering the room. Deep down inside of him he knew he was being tempted, and why, but against that was the desire to work again, to handle delicate equipment and to lose himself in his dream. To build. To construct. To delve into the delicate balance of the human mind and to emulate it in imperishable metal and crystal. He thought of Rosslyn and what he would have said, but Rosslyn was gone, dead, wandering somewhere in the limitless void, and he was alone.

"For peace," he whispered. "Not for war."

"For peace." Almost the man who called himself Smith, smiled, almost, but he knew better than to reveal his triumph. "I promise you."

"And full authority to utilise what material and equipment I need?"

"Yes. There is a base, at the Urals, you will be in sole charge of all scientific work." He leaned forward and rested one thick hand on the scientist's knee. "We need you, Comain, you and men like you. Our wealth is in more than the corn we grow and the metal we dig. It must be in the progress we make, the scientific utilisation of all we possess, the elimination of waste—and war is waste. Will you help, Comain?"

He paused then and silence filled the room, a silence tense with conflicting emotions and opposed loyalties. Comain felt doubt, felt the touch of something sinister, but brushed it aside in the dazzling contemplation of what the big man offered. Tools. Material. Equipment and men. A nation behind him, pressing him on to solve the great problem and resolve his dream. He nodded.

"Good." Smith leaned back and smiled for the first time. "You will never regret this decision." He glanced at his thick left wrist where a thin gold chronometer ticked off the passing minutes. "I shall arrange everything. You understand that it would not be wise to talk of our meeting? They may try to stop you, hold you; even imprison you. They are selfish like that. Even though they do not want you themselves, yet they will kill you to prevent others giving you your opportunity." He rose. "Say nothing. Do nothing. I shall contact you later."

For a moment Comain felt like backing out. For a moment he thought of Rosslyn and what he would have said and done, then as he remembered the wasted years, he hardened himself and banished his doubts.

"I shall be waiting for you," he said quietly. He stared at the big man. "One other thing."

"Yes?"

"The predictor, the machine you want me to build. It may take a little time. In fact it may take a lot of time."

"That doesn't matter." Smith shrugged with elaborate carelessness. "We can wait."

"You may have to wait a long time," repeated Comain. "A very long time."

"It doesn't matter." Smith moved towards the door. "We have time to spare."

He left then, his big figure almost filling the doorway as he left the house and for a long time Comain stared after him.

Then he returned to his books.

CHAPTER VII

Ten million miles beyond Mars, en route to the Red Planet from the Asteroid Belt, a space ship, glinting a little from the weak light of the distant Sun, hung poised against the star-shot night of space. A tiny thing, squat, the stern studded with wide-mouthed venturis, it seemed lifeless and dead, only the starlight winking from its rotating hull betraying the presence of life.

Lars Menson lay in his bunk and stared disgustedly at the smooth metal above his head. Opposite him, seeming to hang from the other side of the compartment like a fly, Jarl Wendis yawned and eased himself into a more comfortable position.

"What's the time, Lars?"

Menson grunted as he twisted and stared at the control panel.

"Twenty hours fifteen minutes and seven seconds. Standard time of course. The month is November and the year, just in case you're interested, is 2210." He scowled at the man opposite. "What the devil do you want to know the time for?"

"No reason." Wendis yawned again. "Just wondering when this trip will be over."

"It'll be over too soon to suit me. Just think of it, Jarl. One more trip after this and we'll be grounded for life."

"Maybe."

"What do you mean, 'maybe'?" Lars stared at the other man. "You know what happens after we get back. The settlement is to be closed and the colonists returned to Earth. We heard the ultimatum just before we took-off."

"We heard what the Matriarch told us would happen," corrected Wendis. "We didn't hear what we were actually going to do." He rose and walked 'down' the wall, the artificial gravity of centrifugal force making every spot on the outer hull 'down'. He sat on the edge of the narrow cot. "Look, Menson," he said quietly. "We don't *have* to do as the Matriarch thinks best you know."

"Rebellion?" Lars smiled and shook his head. "That old dream again? I thought that you had more intelligence than that, Wendis. We wouldn't stand a chance."

"Perhaps not, but then again, perhaps yes."

"What do you mean?"

Wendis shrugged and in the cold glare of the lights his blue eyes were peculiarly intent. Like Menson he was a small man, light boned, slender limbed, and with the well-developed chest and rib case of all the Martian Colonists. Though slender he didn't lack strength, constant exercise and the one-and-a-half times normal Earth gravity maintained within the ship had kept him fit.

"I'm not talking of rebellion," he said quietly. "I've no wish to overthrow the Matriarch. But why should we have to go back to Earth? We're doing all right as we are."

"Didn't you ever go to school?" Menson tried to keep his impatience from his voice. "You know that we are dependent on the home planet for supplies. Ever since the colony was founded, over a hundred years ago now, we have had to rely on Earth for almost everything we need. Even our food has had to come from there. How can we ever be self-sufficient?"

"We could be." Wendis had the stubbornness of the fanatic. "We can get our water from the pole, our food from the yeast vats, our building materials from the oxidised minerals in the sand. We can mine and refine the radioactives, we've been doing that for long enough, and with them we can keep the atomic piles operating to supply light and power. We can even fuel the space ships and mine the Asteroid Belt for rare metals. Damn it, Menson, you know that we can do it."

"I know that we can't do it, and if you'd stop to think about it, so would you." Lars raised himself on one elbow. "As things are now we depend on Earth to buy our asteroid-metal and supply things we can't do without. You talk of living on yeast. Have you ever tried it? Of course you haven't, and if you did, you'd find that within two years you'd be dying of vitamin deficiency. Then what about medical supplies? Drugs? Machine tools? Artefacts? No, Wendis, when you can manufacture a radio from the sand I'll listen to you, not before."

"We can do without radios."

"Agreed. But you're talking of running space ships, and I how can you do that with a technology which can't even make a radio? We could remain on Mars, but if we did, it would I be a primitive existence and we'd be extinct within two generations."

"So you'd rather we crawl back to Earth?"

"What else can we do?" Menson stared at the other man. "Don't get me wrong, Wendis. I want to stay on Mars as I much as you do. It's my home, I was born there and so were my parents, but I don't want to die there fighting a losing battle with the environment. If men could have lived on Mars without outside help they would have done it before this."

"What's wrong with you Menson is that you're a yellow bellied coward!"

"And you're a blind fool."

The two men glared at each other, each fighting his inner rage, and each realising that his rage was only a temporary phase. Spacemen always quarrelled. The free radiations did it, the surging electrons and penetrating gamma particles, disturbing the delicate neuron paths of the brain and triggering quick and sometimes deadly displays of temper.

The barrier screen gave some protection, the steady flow of current within the outer hull, but the screen didn't stop all the radiation, and it couldn't prevent the nervous tension and psychological strain inevitable in the cramped quarters of a space ship.

Men had died for that reason. Died in screaming madness and blood-stained hate. Entire crews had turned, each on the other, and sometimes ships were found manned by a long-dead crew, the inner hull dull with blood and dismembered bodies. Violence when it came had all the ferocity of insanity and civilised decadence.

Menson relaxed, forcing himself to ignore the hate-filled features of the man at his side, and gradually, as it had done before, the tension eased.

"One day I'm going to kill you," said Wendis casually. "I can feel it."

"Then you'll spend the rest of your life regretting it." Menson grinned and glanced at the control panel. "Who would you have to argue with then?"

"I'll get married and take my wife with me. I..." He paused and narrowed his eyes as a red light began to flash its warning signal. "What...?"

"Meteor?" Menson surged from the bunk and slipped into the control seat.

"Could be." Wendis squinted at the radar screen an adjusted the electro-spectroscope. "Pretty big and moving fairly slow." He grunted as he adjusted the controls. Mass about fifty tons. Speed." He pursed his lips. "Relative to us about a hundred and ten." He stared at Menson. "Odd. With that low mass it shouldn't bulk so large."

"Might be hollow. Any chance of a spectro-analysis?"

"Not unless we stop spin and get nearer. Shall we?"

Menson frowned at his controls. "I don't know. Not much chance of getting anything worthwhile so far from the Belt. It's probably just a rogue mass heading for the Sun. Still, it's peculiar that it's so large and so low in mass."

"We could at least see what it's made of," suggested Wendis. "We've plenty of room in the hold and we need all we can get."

"It means free fall." Menson hesitated, his hands resting on the controls. "Can you take it?"

"I've stood it before and I can stand it again. Let's see what it is, Lars. We might be lucky and we can do with all the cash we can get." He grunted with disgust. "We'll probably need it on Earth."

"Right." Menson glanced at the instruments banked over the firing controls and slowly moved a lever down its groove. Sound began to vibrate through the ship, a muffled drumming as of distant rockets, and slowly, so gradually that neither of the men noticed the slightest jerk or strain, the spinning of the vessel died.

With the slowing of the rotation the artificial gravity of centrifugal force died and free fall gripped them with its terrible nausea. Wendis gulped, his thin face pale, and thinned his lips as he squinted through the eyepiece of the spectro-telescope.

"Swing nearer," he grunted. "I can't get a sight."

Menson nodded, staring at the radar detector and letting his hands play over the firing levers. Flame spat from the venturis, jerking them with acceleration surges, and in the tiny circle of the direct vision port something loomed, dark and shapeless against the stars.

"There it is. Can you get a spectro?"

"No heat." Wendis shook his head. "I'll have to warm it up with a tracer."

"Hurry then. I don't want to remain in free fall longer than I have to."

Fire streaked in a thin line from the muzzle of a cannon-like tube mounted beneath the viewing instruments and a tiny, rocket powered projectile, drove towards the mysterious bulk. It hit, exploding into a cloud of incandescent vapour, and Wendis stared thoughtfully at the brilliant lines on the spectroscope screen.

"Any good?"

"I'm not sure," Wendis said slowly. "The spectro shows traces of iron, some copper, a little tungsten and a lot of beryllium. Looks unnatural somehow, too much like an alloy."

"What of it? Fifty tons of beryllium is worth picking up. Get into your suit and make it fast."

"How shall we handle it? Cut it up with the torches, fasten a line, or explode it into an orbit?"

"I'd say fasten a line. We can drag it into an orbit around Mars and send for the tugs. Cutting will take too long and I don't fancy working in free fall."

Wendis nodded and taking a space suit from a locker struggled into the tough fabric and metal. He paused, his helmet still open, and his gloved hands adjusted the controls at his wide belt.

"Testing," he said quietly into the inter-suit radio. "Are you receiving me?"

"Yes." Menson grinned as he replied over the limited channel radio. "Seal up and get moving!"

The hiss of the air lock echoed throughout the ship.

"Am now outside." Wendis's voice came clearly over the radio. "Object about five miles from me. Will use shoulder jets to cross."

"Don't forget your life-line," snapped Menson. "I don't want to have to come out after you as I did on Ceres IV."

"Don't worry," said Wendis grimly. "Once was enough and I might not be so lucky next time." A faint crackle from the radio told of the firing of his shoulder jets and in the tiny circle of the direct vision port twin streamers of fire lanced across the star-shot void.

"See anything?"

"Not yet. I…" Menson heard his startled whistle. "Lars! This isn't a meteor. The shape is too regular."

"What is it then?"

"A ship!"

"What?" Menson leaned closer to the radio. "Are you certain?"

"Don't you think I know what a ship looks like? Of course I'm certain." A soft metallic thud came from the radio. "I've just landed on the hull."

"What identification markings are there? Is it one of ours or one of the Matriarchs?"

"I don't know." Wendis sounded puzzled. "I can't see any markings. I don't even recognise the type of ship, at least, I've never seen one like it before."

"Describe it." Menson tried to keep the impatience from his voice. "What does it look like?"

"About two hundred feet long. Very slender, far too slender to be a cargo vessel. Seven venturis and no steering tubes. Three wide fins. No signs of landing skids or rotating jets. The hull is scarred and split down one side." Wendis gulped. "Menson! This thing is *old*!"

"Are you crazy? How could it be old?"

"I don't know the answer to that one but I do know what radiation does to metal after a century or so. The hull is pitted all over, it's almost rotten, and that means that this ship is an old one." Wendis gulped again. "Menson. Could it be the vessel of an alien race?"

"I doubt it. From what you tell me it sounds like one of the old types, the experimental ones. It's probably a test rocket which somehow got off course."

"I see." Wendis sounded disappointed. "I'd hoped that we'd find something inside, some weapon or machine which could have helped us against the Matriarch. If this is only one of the old automatic rockets it can't be of much value."

"Fifty tons of beryllium are always valuable," reminded Menson. "Fasten the line and get back here."

"Right." Faint noises came from the radio, the transmitted sound of Wendis as he worked on the hull, welding the line to the ancient metal. He grunted, breathing harshly as if exerting all his strength, and Menson frowned as he tried to guess what his partner was doing.

"I'm trying to widen the split in the hull." Wendis sounded irritated at the other's query. "I've fastened the line and with the metal as rotten as it is it shouldn't be hard to lift the outer skin. Anyway, I'm curious to see what's inside." He grunted again as he gripped the jagged edge of the split and tugged at the thin metal.

"Holy Cow!"

"What is it?" Menson's voice rose as he snapped the question. "What have you found?"

"You were wrong, Menson," said Wendis unsteadily. "This wasn't one of the old automatics."

"No? What was it then?"

"A manned rocket ship."

"Impossible. The first manned ships weren't anything like what you described, and anyway, they were all accounted for."

"Not all of them, Menson."

"What do you mean?"

"I mean that someone will have to start revising the history books. This was a manned space ship, and, if I know anything at all about metals, it must be all of two hundred and fifty years old. As far as I know, the first manned ships only reached Mars just over a hundred years ago."

"That's right."

"That's wrong. We can prove it."

"How?"

"With this ship." Wendis sighed, the sound coming clearly over the radio. "It was a manned vessel, there can be no doubt about it, and it must have left Earth more than two centuries ago."

"It couldn't have done. They didn't have the barrier screen then. Are you sure?"

"Yes. It was a manned ship, Lars. I know it. The poor devil is still sitting in his control chair."

"What!"

"Didn't you hear me? The pilot is still inside the ship. Dead of course, frozen, he must have died when the air escaped through the split in the hull, but…" Wendis broke off and Menson reached for the controls.

"Get back here," he snapped. "I'm radioing Mars."

Tensely he adjusted the controls.

CHAPTER VIII

Mars Centre rested on the bed of a long-dried sea three hundred miles from the North Pole. It looked as it had always done, a huddled collection of adobe huts, domed, tamped from the chemical-treated sand of the arid planet. Over the course of the years the settlement had grown, and yet, despite the slow increase of population, the settlement still seemed a rough and temporary affair as if the inhabitants had always known that one day they would have to move.

Five miles from the settlement the squat atomic pile rested, half-buried from the wind-blown dust. From it thick cables snaked to both the settlement and to the idle machines of the refining plant, and the flame-scorched area of the landing field with its high control tower, lay a full mile to the south. Of agricultural land there was no sign, none existed, the sand of Mars, radioactive and sterile couldn't grow a single blade of grass. Instead, the scoured aluminium of the synthetic food plant rose above the clustered domes of the living quarters, and the low building of the one hospital was the second largest building on the entire planet.

Mars was a bleak place.

Doctor Lasser shivered a little as the early chill of night bit through his heavy clothing and gnawed at his fatless body. He was an old man, thin, his gaunt features reflecting something of an inner bitterness, his sunken eyes glinting with a secret torment. He paused for a moment, staring at the sunken ball of the setting Sun, then, shrugging, he thrust himself through the double doors of the hospital.

"Doctor Lasser!" A man stepped towards him from where he stood by two men. "I'm glad you're early."

"Why, Carter? In a hurry to get away?" The old man didn't trouble to hide his sarcasm as he looked at his assistant, the only other doctor on Mars. Carter flushed.

"You misunderstand me, Lasser. Perhaps you'd better reserve your judgment until you hear what these men have to tell you."

"Who are they?"

"Wendis and Menson. Two Asteroid miners. They have only just landed. You must remember their radio message two days ago."

"Yes." Lasser stared at the two men. "When did you arrive?"

"An hour ago." Wendis looked at his partner. "What's all this about a radio message?"

"I told them about what we found." Menson glanced at the tall, thin figure of the old doctor. "Well, Doc? Can it be done?"

Lasser bit his lips. "How can I answer that? I haven't even seen him yet, and anyway, what makes you think that it would be a good idea, even if it were possible?"

"Can there be any doubt?" Carter stared curiously at his chief. "What else can we do? As doctors our duty is clear, and even if we could ignore that duty, there is another reason."

"Yes?"

"If you haven't thought of it for yourself then I'm not telling you." The young man seemed to be on the edge of anger. "What's the matter with you, man? What has changed you in the past few days? I remember the time when you would have been burning with enthusiasm for what we propose."

"You ask me that?" Twin spots of anger burned on the gaunt cheeks and something glowed deep in the sunken eyes "You heard the Matriarch's commands. You heard the ultimatum. Within two weeks we have to evacuate Mars. Within two weeks a hundred years of hope and struggle will be thrown away and forgotten. You know how I feel about that. How can I take an interest in anything now?" He turned away shrugging out of his thick coverall.

"For the younger men the move means nothing. You probably welcome the chance of getting away from here, of going to Earth and all the comfort that planet offers. Things like patriotism, loyalty to old dreams, independence, those things mean nothing to you."

"You are wrong, Lasser, quite wrong." Carter stared at the old man. "We feel just as you do, and if there were a chance, the slightest chance of breaking from the chains of Earth, we would do it. But enough of that now. Will you see him?"

"I suppose I must." Lasser stared at Menson. "Your message stated that you found him in a ship of old design, design obsolete for more than two hundred years. You realise what you are saying of course."

"I do."

"The pilot of that ship has been dead for all that time. He was born before the Atom War, he would know nothing of what has happened since that time, and yet you suggest that we should attempt to revive him."

"Yes."

"Why?"

Menson stared at the old man, half-believing that the doctor was joking. "Are you serious?"

"I am." Lasser sighed a little as he stared at the young miner. "I am an old man, Menson. I see things a little differently than you younger men. Would it be humane to bring him back? He has already known death, have we the right to force him to face it again?"

"I think that we have." Menson stared seriously at the tall doctor. "He died it is true, but it was not a natural death. He must have been a young man when it happened, and, aside from all that, he could tell us a great deal of what happened before the Atom War. I think that you should do what you can."

"I see. Is he here?"

"Yes. We've kept him in cold storage. The ship is in an orbit around Deimos, we can get it if necessary, but I thought that this came first."

"Very well. I will examine him."

Lasser glanced at his assistant and together, the two doctors and the two young Asteroid miners, they left the room and passed into a laboratory almost filled with gleaming apparatus and ranked phials of drugs and surgical instruments. Carefully Carter lifted a sheet from a high-walled vat, and together they stared at what had once been a living man.

"Death was due to asphyxia of course, that and instantaneous freezing as the air in the ship expanded into the void. The wound on his arm is superficial. The blood on his body seems to have come from that wound. Some rupture of the capillaries of course; that would be inevitable from the sudden drop in pressure."

"Do you think that we can revive him?"

"I don't know," said Lasser thoughtfully. "So much depends. If his blood has coagulated, or if his inner organs were ruptured in the pressure drop..." He shrugged. "Men have been revived who have died in space, but for each one who has been brought back to life two others have died under the treatment. Also, and we mustn't forget this, he has been exposed to the free radiations of space for over two centuries. They must have affected him in some way; how, we can't even guess, but it makes a new variable, an unknown factor."

"The time element isn't too important," protested Carter. "Space is sterile, and, when he died, his every cell froze solid. There couldn't have been any deterioration, as we see him so he was on the day of his death."

"Aside from the radiation effects," reminded Lasser quietly. "But I agree with you about the lack of deterioration." He sighed and glanced at the other men. "Well, we may as well get started. The usual procedure?" Carter nodded.

"Yes. Immersion in a temperature controlled fluid. Slow thawing to prevent internal damage. Eddy currents and electronic surge pulses to ensure even heating. Energen flow to revive the individual cell-life. Stimulants for the heart, artificial breathing, heart massage, the whole procedure. We may fail, but if we don't…"

"A dead man will live again." Lasser glanced at the two Asteroid miners. "You had better return to your duties. This will take some time, we shall have to be careful in arousing his mental awareness; shock could kill him beyond recall." Wendis hesitated, and Menson looked at Carter.

"I want them to stay here," said the young doctor evenly. "Now that the ultimatum expires within two weeks there is no point in them continuing with their work." He hesitated glancing at the old man. "I can use them here anyway," he said abruptly. "We have a lot to do before we leave."

Lasser nodded, not really caring what happened now that his life-long dream of an independent Mars was at an end, and stooped his thin figure over the high-walled vat.

Delicately he fingered the cold flesh, the iron hard, solidly frozen flesh of a man who had been dead for almost a century and a half. Carefully he switched on a power source, adjusting a row of controls and slowly opening a valve.

"Head support and mask."

Carter adjusted a support beneath the dead man's head and strapped a mask over the contorted features. "Ready." Lasser nodded and from the valve beneath his hand spurted a stream of iridescent green liquid. Lights flickered over a panel, and from a squat machine came the smooth hum of power beneath perfect control.

The battle for life had started.

It took three days. Three days in which the temperature of the green liquid slowly rose to well above blood heat, in which the invisible surges of electronic eddy currents warmed the dead body through and through, melting the buried specks of ice within each cell, thawing the dead flesh and relaxing the stiffened limbs. Machines hummed into life at the exact moment they were needed. The artificial lungs pumped almost pure oxygen into the flaccid chest, the loaded hypodermics with their cargoes of stimulants for nerves and muscles.

Carter never left the side of the vat. He crouched over the controls of the energen generator, adjusting the flow of the current which emulated life itself, restoring vitality and individual life to each cell.

Still the body didn't respond.

Lasser stared down at the vat, his thin features drawn and almost haggard with strain and worry. Before him, totally immersed in the shimmering green liquid, the dead man seemed to live with a travesty of life. The chest rose and fell, impelled by the artificial lung. The blood circulated, forced by the devices which by-passed the natural organ. Almost it seemed as if the man would rise and throw off the mask and tubes attached to his body, but the old doctor knew that once the machines stopped, the man would truly die, and this time there would be no second chance.

"How is the energen content?"

"At normal, plus ten percent, for extra stimulus." Carter wearily rubbed his tired eyes. "Body heat one hundred degrees, saline content normal, circulation increased by fifteen percent, air almost pure oxygen. Damn it all, Lasser. The man should be alive by now."

"Muscular reaction?" The old man ignored his assistant's outburst.

"Motor nerves respond. Involuntary reactions absent."

"I see." Lasser thinned his lips as he stared into the vat. "Expose the heart," he snapped. "We'll try direct massage and electro-shock treatment. If we don't get him breathing beneath his own power soon we may as well give up. Deterioration in the motor nerves must already have commenced. We daren't wait any longer."

Carter nodded and reached for a heavy scalpel.

It took ten hours. Ten hours in which the old doctor's hands within their sterile gloves kneaded the exposed heart of the dead man, massaging it in time to the pulse of the blood pump. Carter hovered over him, ready to take over should Lasser weary of the delicate task, injecting stimulants into the muscle and keeping a watchful eye on the bank of flickering dials.

Finally the heart pulsed, stopped, beat again, then, fitfully at first but with increasing power, it took over the task of the blood pump. Wearily Lasser leaned back and watched as Carter sewed back the flap of bone and muscle.

"At least his body is living," he said tiredly. "Now, unless the shock of death has affected his mind, he should recover."

"Shall I disconnect the artificial lung?"

"Not yet. We must relieve his heart as much as possible until his own lungs regain awareness. That is the next job."

"Shock treatment?"

"No. I don't like it, there is too much danger of damaging the brain. Use pain and direction. You know what to do." The old man slowly stripped the gloves from his hands. "Call me when he recovers."

Carter nodded, already at work on the problem of awakening the dormant memory and awareness of the man in the vat.

Always there was this problem. Death seemed to be something more than just the stopping of the heart. The delicate, almost immeasurable electrical potential of the brain, played a still larger part. Men, once they knew that they had died, were impossible to revive. There was a mental refusal to accept awareness, and so, even though their bodies lived, their brains did not, and without that personal awareness they remained mindless idiots, or lapsed again into oblivion.

"Who are you?" Carter spoke into a microphone, his words drumming against the ears of the man in the vat, carried through the earpieces of the mask covering the man's head. As he asked the question he pressed a button and electricity stabbed at the sensory nerves of the dead brain.

"Who are you?" Again the question and again the stabbing flow of current. "Who are you? Who are you? Who are you?"

It went on for hours. It went on until Carter hated the sound of his own voice, until his face and neck dripped with sweat, and his fingers trembled with weariness as they adjusted the controls. He didn't expect an answer. He didn't hope for anything better than that the man should answer his call and struggle up from his oblivion to an unconscious awareness of life.

"Who are you?"

A direct appeal to the ego. A challenge to the self. A call from light and life into the darkness of death.

"Who are you?"

Gently Carter slowed, then stopped the smooth rhythm of the artificial lung. If the man was going to live he would do so now, and the sooner he could take over the natural functions of his body the better. Staring at him Carter felt a swift panic as the even rise and fall of the chest stopped, stopped, hesitated, then, erratically, began to rise and fall again.

The man breathed.

Quickly he stripped off the mask, transferring the earphones, and a fresh urgency came into his voice as he repeated the monotonous question.

"Who are you?"

The man writhed, his mouth twisting and his arms threshing at his sides.

"Who are you?"

"Ro..." The man's voice trailed away into a gurgling silence.

"Who are you?"

"L... Y... N..." It was like a cracked record, grating and filled with some terrible pain. The man writhed again, his lips parting, his muscles quivering to the twin stimuli of voice and surging current.

"Rosslyn... Rosslyn... Rosslyn."

Carter grunted with satisfaction and triumph, but he had to make quite certain, he had to be cruel now so that the fact of his own identity would remain in the man's pain-twisted brain. He reached for the button controlling the electric current.

"Who are you?"

"Rosslyn..." A terrible fatigue seemed to drain the voice of all vitality. Carter bit his lip and twisted the control of the energen generator.

"Who are you?"

"Rosslyn. Curt Rosslyn. Leave me alone will you. Leave me alone."

Carter smiled and gently took the earphones from the sagging head. Carefully he adjusted the limp body, making sure that the retaining straps held the man so that he could do lf no harm, then, leaving the sterilizing lamps blazing down on the vat, left the room.

"Rosslyn," he murmured as he walked towards Lasser room. "I wonder who he was?"

Tiredly he summoned his relief.

CHAPTER IX

Curt Rosslyn sat in a chair and stared with wondering eyes at the sandy wastes of Mars. Before him, clear through the transparent plastic of the hospital dome, the settlement sprawled, the narrow streets thronged with busy men and women, as they made last-minute preparations for the evacuation. A ground car churned down the street, dust pluming from beneath its treads, and Lasser, his thin body muffled in his coverall, plunged towards the building. Carter followed him, and Curt, still weak even after ten days beneath the healing lamps of the hospital, waited impatiently for them enter the room.

"Well, Curt?" Carter smiled as he brushed dust from his coverall. "How are you feeling today?"

"Not too bad, but my chest is still sore."

"Not surprising when you consider that we had to remove half the rib case in order to massage your heart." Lasser sighed as he slumped into a chair. The old man seemed to have aged in the past ten days, his eyes glowed from their sunken pits, and his parchment-like skin had an unhealthy flush. "Well, fit or not, you'll have to move tomorrow."

"So soon?" Curt stared again at the wastes of Mars. "Must we? Wouldn't it be possible for me to see the planet first?" He smiled apologetically at the old man. "Remember, I was only trying to reach the Moon when…" He faltered and Carter nodded with quiet understanding.

"I know how you feel, Curt, but you must try to accept what happened. You died on that trip, you know that, but if you let yourself refuse to accept the fact it will cause a psychological trauma which could lead to grave trouble."

"Thanks," said Curt, and took a deep breath. "Well then. I died before I could ever reach the Moon, and at that time a journey to Mars was just something we dreamed of. Now, when by a miracle I am really here, it seems that I'm never going to see it at all. Can't you delay the evacuation?"

"No," snapped Lasser, and Curt flushed.

"Maybe I shouldn't have asked," he said quietly. "I forget, you wouldn't understand just how I feel about some things."

"Don't misunderstand him, Curt." Carter rose and stared out of the transparency of the dome. "If Lasser had his way he would never leave here, none of us would, but we have no choice."

"Because of the supply position?"

"Yes. You know about that?"

"Menson told me. But I can't understand it all. You've been here for over a hundred years and the settlement must have cost billions to establish. I realise that perhaps it can't pay its way, but to abandon everything just doesn't make sense. Why don't they send you enough equipment to make the colony self-supporting?"

"Why?" Lasser glared at the young man. "I'll tell you why. They don't want us here that's why. They want us back on Earth, back where they can control us as they control everyone else. Out here we're too independent and the Matriarch doesn't like it."

"The Matriarch?" Curt frowned and looked at Carter. "I'm afraid that there's a lot I'll have to catch up on. When I..." He paused again, then almost defiantly uttered the word. "When I died there was no Matriarchy. Do you mean that the women rule now?"

"Yes." Carter turned from the window with a strange weariness. "The women took over after the Atom War, that must have been about twenty years after your death. One of the Eastern Groups of nations unleashed the fury of atomic weapons. The West succumbed of course, they didn't have a chance, but it was a useless victory. They had used radioactive dusts and they spread, drifting on the winds and carried by the rains, and the victor suffered as much as the vanquished. They say that over a thousand million people died and for a long time afterwards most of the fertile soil remained a radioactive desert."

"So it came," whispered Curt sickly. "We had been afraid of it even in my own time. But how did that make the women rulers?"

"For a long time, I think it must have been about fifty years, men suffered a peculiar form of debility. Boy children were more susceptible to mutational changes than girl children, and the mortality rate was three to one in favour of the girls. Naturally, with a predominance of women and a race of men who were weak and cursed with a poor physical and mental heritage from the effects of the selective radiations, a Matriarchy was inevitable. The sex balance equalised itself of course, men are no longer weak, but the old forms die hard."

"It isn't just that, Carter." Lasser thrust himself forward as he stared at his assistant. "A Matriarchy isn't so bad in itself, though women make poor rulers, but it isn't just habit that keeps them in control."

"I know that, but even with what they have we could still overthrow them."

"Do you want to?" Curt stared at the two men. "Surely that is going a little too far? I realise how you must feel at being forced to leave your homes but is that reason for wishing rebellion?"

"Rebellion?" Lasser smiled, a curious grimace without a trace of humour. "No, Curt, we aren't talking of armies and guns, of fleets and civil war. We talk of a rebellion of ideals, a lifting of the blanket which is stifling ambition and progress." He pointed towards the desert. "Look out there. For more than a hundred years we have tried to turn this planet into a place where men could live, and we have failed. Another thing, space travel has been known, really known I mean, for two hundred years now. The first observatory on the moon was built there fifty years before we reached Mars. Since that time we have advanced no further. We have settled on Mars, touched Venus, approached Mercury—and that is all."

"All?" Curt frowned. "But with all that time for progress…"

"Exactly." Lasser glared in triumph. "We should have reached Pluto by now, developed a stardrive, thrust ourselves towards the new worlds waiting beyond Pluto and founded colonies of men on Alpha Centauri. We have done none of those things."

"But why not?"

"Comain." Lasser spat the word as if it were a curse.

"What!" Curt lunged forward in his chair, then, as his sore chest protested against his movements, winced and leaned back again. "Comain. Can he be still alive? I knew him, we were friends, what has he to do with this?"

"He?" Lasser frowned. "What are you talking about?"

"Comain of course. You mentioned him. Is he still alive?"

"He? I'm not talking about a man."

"Then…" Curt stared helplessly at the old man, conscious as he had been a thousand times of all he did not know, of the terrible gap which lay between him and these others, a gap of two and a-half centuries. Carter turned from where he stared out of the dome and looked at the young man.

"Comain is a *machine*," he explained quietly. "A vast machine which literally controls the destiny of Earth and every living man and woman on it. The Matriarch depends on it for everything, and that is why we must return to Earth."

"A machine!" Curt sagged in his chair. "I had hoped…" He shook his head. "Funny. Comain was the last person I spoke to before the automatics fired and the hull split open. I'd been cursing him for his faulty design; I wish that I hadn't now, it wasn't really his fault." He stared at Carter. "But why, Comain? Why call a machine after a man?"

Carter shrugged. "Probably because of the man who invented it. Legend has it that he lived before the Atom War, and that his machine was the cause of the holocaust. The attacking nations financed him, and he and his devil's machine predicted that they would win the battle. He…" The young man broke off conscious for the first time of what he was saying. "Comain. You said that you knew him. Lasser, did you hear that?"

"I did." The old man stared hungrily at Curt. "You knew him you say? You *knew* him?"

"I knew a man named Comain. We grew up together, went to school together; tried for the stars as though we were one."

"Could it be possible? And yet, why not? It was a miracle that we found you, revived you, and why not yet a third coincidence? You are certain that you knew Comain?"

"Yes." Curt flushed as he glared at the old man. "I knew him well. He was a clever man and he often spoke of the value of cybernetics. I remember, it may have been just before I left for the Moon, that he spoke of a machine which could assimilate data and extrapolate from it and form a prediction of high probability. It wasn't a new idea, but he had definite lines on which he proposed working as soon as he could obtain the backing and facilities." He stared at the tense faces of the two men. "Anyway, is it so important?"

"It could be," said Carter slowly, and he looked at the old man with a strange expression. "I had a vague idea when we found you that in some way you might be of use to us, but now..." He narrowed his eyes in thought and began striding about the domed chamber. "Lasser! Can we get him Earth unsuspected?"

"I don't know." The old man stared at Curt with hooded eyes. "Why?"

"You know how Comain works. Within its memory banks reposes the sum total of all knowledge and information known to Man. More than that, it has checked and registered every living person on Earth and on Mars. Everyone, remember, everyone."

"So?"

"Its predictions are based on a multiplicity of factors. The age, height, sex, colouration, peculiarities, ESP factor, of everyone. *Everyone* remember. It has full details of everything known, data to the square of almost infinity. That is why the Matriarch wants us back on Earth. We are too independent here, too liable to do the unpredictable. Comain doesn't have enough information on us, on Mars, on space even to form more than a sixty percent prediction on what we may do. That must affect the predictions on Earth. Remote though we are yet we must affect the probability factor enough to leave a margin of doubt. Once we are on Earth, beneath the auspices of Comain, then the predictions will be almost nine nines percent probable. In other words the Matriarch will know the result of every action, every decision, every experiment she wishes, and know it before it happens."

"I know all that," snapped Lasser impatiently. "It is merely a question of simple mathematics. If a man, or a machine, could know everything, then, from that knowledge, it or he could predict what must happen from any interaction." He snorted with humourless laughter. "It could even predict what must happen in the future, and, so dependent are those fools of Earth on Comain, that they will bring its prophecies to fulfilment merely because they believe that what is predicted must be true, and so will make it so by their own actions." He stared at Curt. "Can you follow all this?"

"I think so. We had something like it in our own time, and something like it has always existed. The high priests of primitive tribes did it, and so did the witch doctors of a later era. They would tell a man that he would die, and, because the man believed that what the witch doctor said was truth, he did die." Curt shrugged. "It was psychology of course, the man really died because he convinced himself that he had to die. The spell never worked unless the subject had faith in the witch doctor."

"Comain hardly deals in psychology," said Lasser dryly "If it predicts that a man will die, then that man *will* die, and he needn't even know anything about the prediction at all. Comain deals in hard facts, not dubious mumbo-jumbo."

"Perhaps," said Curt easily. "But faith, whether in man or machine, can do peculiar things."

"Yes," said Carter sombrely. "It is forcing us to evacuate Mars."

He stared out of the dome again, his eyes clouded as he watched the scurrying figures below, and Curt had the impression of subtle undercurrents and hidden stresses. He shifted uneasily in his chair, wishing that he were wholly well, and within his skull his brain seemed to burn with strange fires.

"Well, Carter? Have you decided what to do with our friend?" Lasser sighed as he relaxed in his chair, a bitter expression in his sunken eyes. Slowly the young doctor turned from the darkening scene outside.

"Can we get him to Earth without the knowledge of Comain?"

"I suppose so," snapped Lasser impatiently. "We have all been registered here, the Matriarch saw to that, and they know just how many of us will return to Earth. Why?"

"I have an idea," said Carter slowly. "An insane idea perhaps, but what else have we to try? Listen. Suppose we did get Curt back to Earth without the knowledge of Comain. He hasn't been registered, nothing is known about him, and yet, by his mere presence, he must affect the actions of others." He stared at the old man. "Now do you understand?"

"No. I...." Lasser paused, and on his thin lips hovered the ghost of a smile. "Yes. By all the Gods of Space, Carter! Will it work?"

"Will what work?" Curt looked at them, frowning, a little uneasy, but they ignored him, too occupied in their own plans. "It all depends on whether or not we can get him back without discovery. We can swear the others to secrecy, Wendis and Menson will have to be careful, they must dodge re-registration, we can tell the others that he died."

"Yes, that shouldn't be difficult." Lasser licked his thin lips with a nervous gesture. "Now. The Matriarch's ships will land tomorrow. They will have the normal crew, a single metaman to each ship. We could hide him in a bale or something and smuggle him out at the other end." He frowned at Carter. "The whole thing depends on whether or not Comain will check us on arrival, and, if I know the Matriarch, that will be one of the first things to happen."

"Why should it be?" Curt half-rose from his chair, ignoring the pain stabbing at his sore chest. "I thought that you'd already been registered?"

"We have," said Carter dryly. "But Lasser is right, the Matriarch will insist on us going before Comain as soon as we land. They will have to integrate our data into the overall pattern or the whole reason for our recall will be rendered invalid."

"Well? Need you tell of my existence?"

"We can't hide it once we go before Comain." Carter sounded worried. "The machine can read our minds you know, or rather you don't know, but it can and that makes it impossible to lie to it."

"Read your minds?" Curt slumped back in his chair, conscious again of the terrible gap in his knowledge. "How can it do that?"

"Transference of the electro-potential of the neuronic currents in the brain." The young man smiled briefly at Curt's blank expression. "Thought is electrical, a fine mesh of differing electric potential, measurable, and varying from individual to individual. Somehow, I don't pretend to know how, Comain can transfer a copy of that potential to its own memory banks. That means that it knows everything the subject knows. The process is painless, almost instantaneous, and, thanks to the Matriarch, unavoidable."

"I see." Curt frowned down at his interlaced fingers. "Couldn't you beat the machine in some way? Use hypnotism for example?"

"Hypnotism?" Carter stared blankly at the young man. "What is that?"

"Don't you know?" Curt didn't trouble to hide his surprise. Do you mean to say that you've never heard of it? You, a medical man?"

"I know what he means," said Lasser. The old man stared at his assistant and his sunken eyes burned with a strange fire. "Auto-suggestion induced while in a trance-state. You wouldn't know of it, but a long time ago its use was quite common. I learned how to induce it when a young student, but it can be dangerous and was barred by the medical facility about a century and a half ago." He smiled faintly at man in the chair. "You can understand how the mere fact of it being forbidden tended to make certain young men eager to dabble in it."

"Yes, but can you do as I suggested?"

"I think so. Wendis and Menson will have to be treated of course. Luckily they are the only ones other than ourselves who know of you. Menson had the good sense not to babble to the radio operator when he reported to Carter what he had found."

"Then we can do it?" Carter seemed almost consumed with an inner eagerness. "We can smuggle our extra man Earth without Comain knowing of his existence?"

"I think so." Lasser nodded and his thin lips writhed in a humourless smile. "We will have to take all precautions course, use a post-hypnotic suggestion to enable us to remember him after we have passed through Comain, but I think that it can be done."

"I hope so." Curt eased his aching chest. "I'd hate you to forget all about me after we land. From what you tell me things are a lot different from what they were when I left."

"Yes," said Carter quietly. "Things are different. A lot different, but they will differ again after you have landed." He looked at the old man and his laughter rang loud against the encroaching silence of the night. "Wait until he begins upsetting all their clever little predictions. Just wait until we introduce our extra man to the water-tight society of Earth."

Lasser nodded, his thin features sombre, and his eyes glowing against the pallor of his withered cheeks.

"The extra man," he murmured softly. "Yes. I like that, a good name to call him, a safe name. An extra man, and with luck, and if we have guessed right, he may win Mars for us. An independent Mars, free of the Matriarch and of Comain."

Curt shivered at the naked emotion in the old man's voice.

CHAPTER X

Sarah Bowman, Matriarch of Earth, stood at a high window and stared down at the concrete perfection of the building which was Comain.

Five thousand feet the building soared, rising like an artificial mountain from the flat plain below. Spired, terraced, sweeping in subtle curves and arching beauty, rising like something from an old tale, a fairy palace, a mound in which art and science had met and blended in enduring steel and stone. And yet this was not Comain.

Far down, buried beneath a shielding layer of rock and lead, soil and running water, protected from high explosive and atomic destruction, from radiation and natural storm, the machine which was Comain rested as it had rested for more than two centuries. An incredible complexity of crystal and wire, of tube and relay, of warped atoms and strained molecules, the swollen fruit of one man's genius rested, and, as if they were inexhaustible sponges, the ranked tiers of its memory banks absorbed every minute scrap of knowledge available to the minds of men.

Such was Comain.

For a long time the Matriarch stood at the high window and stared down at the terraced building, then, sighing a little, she turned and moved towards the centre of the huge office. A desk rested by the window, a wide thing of superb polish and immaculate workmanship, its surface littered now with sheaves of papers and squat, portable filing cabinets. Against one wall the blank face of a video screen reflected little shimmers of light from the dying light outside the window, and the smaller, darker screens of several videophones stared like blind eyes towards the wide desk.

The room was very quiet.

Heavily the Matriarch slumped into her chair, and, for a moment, sat staring down at her thick, broad nailed, swollen knuckled fingers. She was an old woman, her close-cropped hair white with age, and her heavy, almost mannish features seamed and wrinkled, the lips bloodless, the eyes surrounded by a multitude of tiny lines. She wore not the slightest trace of cosmetics, and, sitting at the wide desk, her shapeless body hidden in a simple dress of dull grey, she seemed like an old and weary man. It was only when emotion aroused her and her eyes flashed with an almost forgotten fire, that she resembled the militant female who had climbed her way to the highest pinnacle of government.

But that had been long ago.

A bell chimed in the office, its muted tone sounding strangely loud in the deepening twilight, and one of the videophone screens flared with a sudden swirl of light, steadying into a coloured picture of a middle aged woman.

"Madam?"

"Yes?" The Matriarch stared towards the screen. "What is it?"

"Your secretary, Madam. May she enter?"

"Admit her." The picture dissolved into a swirl of colour and the screen returned to its normal darkness. At the same time, operated by the light-sensitive selenium cells, the room lights glowed into soft radiance.

Softly the door opened and a woman entered the room.

She was tall and with a curved slenderness and as she walked towards the wide desk her figure moved with the innate grace of a dancer. Unlike the Matriarch she wore a clinging dress of some iridescent black material elaborately worked in a pattern of golden arabesques. Long hair, black as jet, flowed from her high forehead and fell in smooth ripples to her sloping shoulders. Her skin was a milky white, like whipped cream or white velvet, and her eyes were slanted pools of midnight beneath thick brows.

"Good evening, Madam."

The old woman grunted, her broad nostrils twitching at subtle aroma of perfume. "You may sit, Nyeeda."

"Thank you." The secretary smoothed her dress as she sat in a vacant chair. "Have you finished your study of the agricultural figures, Madam?"

"No, they can wait."

"As you decide. They aren't important anyway, we know to within five percent, just what the yield will be."

"We knew that last year, before the crops were even planted, but I suppose that I have to go through the motions of checking the figures." The old woman sighed as she stared at the heaped papers on her desk. "Have the Martians arrived yet?"

"Not yet. They are orbiting at the moment and will land within an hour from now." Nyeeda stared a little curiously at the old woman. "Don't you remember the prediction? Comain gave the flight schedule and landing times."

"Of course I remember, but it had slipped my mind. Anyway, these details aren't important."

"All details are important." The girl spoke with a flat conviction. "The more data we can feed into Comain the more accurate its predictions will be. I thought that was the whole idea of bringing the colonists back to Earth."

"It is. While the activities of an independent group have to be considered the predictions cannot be as accurate as we would wish. You don't have to instruct me on the basics of our civilisation, Nyeeda. I learned them long before you were born."

"Yes, Madam, I am sorry."

"Forget it, girl, you are too young to have to apologise to an old woman, and you have been with me too long for us to misunderstand each other. How long is it now? Fifteen years?"

"Not quite. I've been your personal secretary for ten years now, ever since I graduated from general duties."

"Of course. I remember now, Comain selected you as being the one person most suited to my needs. As usual the prediction was right, I've had no cause for complaint."

"Thank you, Madam." Nyeeda smiled and relaxed in her chair.

"Not that I approve of women in governmental positions using cosmetics, perfume, wearing jewellery and expensive clothes. But then, you are young, and as you grow older you will realise that these things pass along with other childish amusements." The old woman shrugged as she spoke and the gesture robbed her tone of offence. "Now, about these Martians. They will be registered on landing of course, all five hundred and seventy two of them. I trust that the necessary orders have been given?"

"The metamen at the landing field have their instructions. They will conduct the colonists to the booths directly they leave the ships. The prediction is five nines against violence of any kind."

"Good. Has it been decided just what they are to do and where to live?"

"Not yet. It was thought best to leave those details until after they had registered with Comain. The extra data will be essential if they are to be fitted in with maximum worth to society."

"I see. Has the Council any ideas on the subject?"

"A few minutes were devoted to discussing the problem but it was felt that any further discussion would be a waste of time. Comain will decide as it must anyway."

"Yes," said the old woman heavily. "Of course." She bit her lips as she stared at the litter of papers on her desk. "Tell me, Nyeeda," she said quietly. "Have you ever thought that at times we tend to place too much reliance on Comain?"

"Why, no. Comain is efficient, we all know that, and not to use it would be utterly illogical." Nyeeda frowned as s looked at the Matriarch. "You surprise me, Madam. You were one of the foremost to advocate the full use of Comain. It was you who ruled that all governmental positions should filled by selection, and now it is Comain who selects the rulers not the people."

"I know that." The old woman spoke with a surprising sharpness. "That was my first ruling when I finally won to Matriarchy. I did it because even then, even though we had used the benefits of Comain for almost two centuries, the old political squabbling and manoeuvring still squandered our time and effort. That was a long time ago now, more than fifty years, and I swore to do it when my political rival, Lucy Armsmith, committed suicide after my election. She was a great woman, but she couldn't stand defeat."

"Nothing like that could happen now," said Nyeeda with quiet certainty. "The predictions of the machine are getting more and more accurate. A person would be an insane fool to try and go against them. If Comain predicts defeat then the person concerned doesn't even argue about it, he just gives up and tries something else."

"I'm glad to hear you say that, Nyeeda, very glad." Something in the old woman's tones made the young girl glance at her with shocked suspicion. The Matriarch saw her expression, and shook her head. "No, girl, I'm not getting senile, just old, and when a person gets old their viewpoint can alter. When I was a girl I lived by Comain, nothing was clearer than that it should be allowed to control the world. I was an idealist I suppose, but the young are always idealists."

"There is nothing wrong in that."

"No, but just lately, I have begun to wonder whether or not I did right. The predictions are getting more and more accurate, and, as they show a higher percentage of probability, more and more people are doing exactly as Comain says they will do. They do it, and by so doing ensure that the prediction is correct. In a way it is a vicious circle, and sometimes, when I am alone and the world is dark, it almost frightens me."

"Frightens you?" Nyeeda laughed. "What a peculiar notion. Surely, Madam, you must be joking?"

"No. I am not joking."

"Then…"

"Listen, Nyeeda. I'm an old woman, over eighty years old and even with the progress geriatrics has made, that is still old. I have seen a great deal of change in the fifty years that I have been the Matriarch. There is not the struggle there used to be, the striving; the ambition. Now people seem to be easily contented, they do as the machine predicts, and it has been ten years since a request was made for restricted information. We are safe from war, from famine, from actual want, but, in gaining all that, have we lost something?"

"If losing the desire to wage war is loss then we may have done." Nyeeda didn't trouble to hide her contempt. "Always there has been this looking backward to the 'good old days.' Even as a girl I remember my father regretting the old times when a man could do as he wanted when he wanted. He used to read old books, books describing wars and armoured men fighting with swords. He even made such a weapon, but of course he never used it for anything but to cut down weeds. He was a dreamer, content with the benefits of civilisation and pretending to long for the hardships he had never known."

"And you think that I am like that?" The Matriarch shook her head. "No, Nyeeda, I am not a fool. I do not want the old days of toil and want to return, but there is something else, a subtle intangible something which mankind always had and which I am afraid he may have lost. I refer to ambition."

"A man can advance himself, earn money, live richly and well. There are still opportunities."

"Are there? I doubt it. Now, if a man thinks of a thing to do, he refers it to Comain. If the prediction is favourable he does it, but he has no vest in what he does. Why should he? He knows before he starts that what he proposes will succeed. Now we have no failures, no lost causes, no battling hopelessly against fate and overwhelming odds."

"Why should we? A failure is effort wasted."

"Agreed, but it wasn't always so. Men reached for planets against all the predictions of logic and common sense. They died because of that dream, but they finally won through. Would we do that now?"

"Would we wear skins and eat raw meet? Would we use flint and steel to kindle a fire or pray to pagan Gods?" Nyeeda shook her head. "You know the answer to that, and the answer to your own question must be the same. Why should we? What need is there to reach for the stars? We have our civilisation, it is a good one, and the people are happy. Let them remain so. What sense is there in idle fears and empty longing. We are what we are, our civilisation what it is, the past is dead and forgotten."

Silence followed her words, and in the silence the sound of the Matriarch's heavy breathing sounded oddly loud. Against the night shrouded window the thin trails of stratoliners traced their fiery paths across the sky and far below, on the level plain surrounding the building, lights sparkled and shimmered in colourful array.

"Thank you, Nyeeda." The old woman smiled and something seemed to relax her thick-set figure. "I knew that I was right, but age, and the chilling of youthful ambition had made me doubt myself. What you say is true, we are safe now and divorced from the strains which lead to war. Now that the Martians have been recalled we can forget the unknown factor and the predictions will be accurate to nine nines percent. Comain will assimilate their data, decide where they are to live and work, and the whole business of space travel can be refiled in the restricted information area of the machine. It will be there if ever we need it, but I doubt if we ever will. No.

I was a fool to worry. Everything will work out as planned. Comain will guide us, save us from false decisions, and, as you mentioned, take over the governing powers."

Slowly she rose from behind the wide desk and crossed to the high window.

"Earth will be a paradise," she whispered. "The Matriarchy will remain the nominal head of state but all decisions will, as now, be referred to Comain. Once the Martians have been registered it will be inevitable. Nothing can prevent it."

Against the night slender tongues of flame stabbed from the heavens and a thin whistling roar began to drone softly through the silent room. The drone increased, the scintillating tongues of fire grew more brilliant, and the Matriarch sighed as she watched them.

"The Martians," she murmured quietly. "Coming home." Nyeeda nodded, crossing to the high window, and together the two women, one old, the other still young, watched the descending space ships.

CHAPTER XI

Five men sat in a room and discussed their future. Carter, his young features taunt with the effort necessary to move his body in a, to him, three times normal gravity, slumped in a chair and stared at the sagging cheeks of the old doctor. Wendis and Menson, used to a high G field while in space, didn't seem to be affected by the gravity, though they gasped and sweated in the thick, humid air. Curt smiled as he stared through a window, savouring the green fields and blue sky, his healed body tingling with excitement as he thought of the new world waiting for his exploration.

"I've heard from the Matriarch," said Lasser bitterly. "As I suspected they have dismantled the ships. We are here to stay."

Wendis clenched his big hands. "That means that we never go into space again, never see the cold stars; feel the thrust of rockets." He swallowed as if ashamed of his outburst, then, almost defiantly, stared at the old doctor. "I've trained all my life for space," he gritted. "I know nothing else. What they intend doing with me now?"

"The Council will inform me as soon as they receive the answer from Comain." Lasser wiped sweat from his yellowed features. "If you ask me to make a guess I'd say either the deserts, the poles, or, if they have work there, on a high mountain."

"What makes you say that, Doc?"

"Logic, Menson. We need a dry climate, low gravity, and thin, cold air. The only place on Earth where we can get most of those things is on a high mountain. The isolation wouldn't worry us, we're used to it, and, from their point of view, it would be ideal."

"Why?"

"We'd be out of the way, and yet under constant observation. Without ships or transport we couldn't leave the area and we'd have to do as we were told or our supplies could be cut off."

"Do you think that they will keep us together?" Carter licked his lips as he looked at the old man. "I thought that they might have split us up, a family here, a man there, and so on."

"Why should they? We aren't rebels. They have nothing to fear from us. They only recalled us so that we could be fitted into the pattern. No, Carter, I think that they will keep us as a unit. All of us."

"What about Curt?"

"Well? What about me?" Attracted by the mention of his name the young man turned from the window and smiled down at the old doctor. "I'm home again, thanks to you, and I'm eager to explore. What happens now?"

"We don't know yet, not until the Matriarch informs me just what is to happen to us." Lasser wiped his face and neck as he glanced up at the young man. "How are you feeling?"

"Fine." Curt grinned as he thumped his chest. "All the soreness has gone and I feel like a dog with two tails."

"Good. Got over the journey yet?"

"Just about. I don't want to do it again though. The trip here wasn't too bad, that dope you gave me knocked me out and sent some beautiful dreams, but I had a bad time after we landed wondering whether or not you'd remember about me."

"You won't have to do it again," said Wendis grimly. Mankind has made the last space trip."

"Maybe." Curt shrugged and looked at the old doctor. "How did the registration go?"

"As I suspected. The metamen were waiting for us and took us directly to the booths. Comain assimilated our data and is probably working on the problem now."

"So long?" Curt stared his surprise.

"No. The machine can't volunteer information. It has to wait until the right question is asked. The Council are probably doing that right now."

"I see." The young man wandered over to the window and nodded towards a tremendous building, bright in the morning sun. "Is that it?"

"That's Comain, the main part of it anyway. The upper building is composed of governmental offices and living quarters. The palace you might say. The priestly apartments to the *Deus Machina*." Wendis sounded bitter.

Curt ignored the other man's tone. He stared at the tremendous building, admiring its smooth perfection and subtle curves, trying to visualise the man who had been his friend, the man who had laid the foundations of this new civilisation. Memory tugged at the innermost chambers of his mind. A man stepped from the mists of the past, a tall man, thin, with weak eyes and gaunt features. He smiled, a semi-ironical twisting of his lips, and a ghost-voice echoed from the ghost-body.

"Hello, Curt."

"Comain."

"It's been a long time, Curt. Sorry about that hatch."

"Comain!"

"We must get together sometime. You know where I live?"

"Yes. Yes, I…" Something jarred him. Something stung his face and pain seared its way through the mists of his mind. Pain. Pain and something more than pain, and he turned, his hands clenching and lifting in sudden rage.

"Curt! Snap out of it man! What's the matter with you?" Carter stood before him, his hand still lifted, ready to slap again.

"You…" Curt swung, his fist driving to the other's mouth, and before the young doctor could ward the blow Curt repeated it, feeling a hot tide of rage warm his stomach as he battered at the other's features.

"Curt! You fool! Stop it!" Wendis lunged forward. Menson behind him, and together they held his arms. Carter dabbed at his damaged mouth.

"Snap out of it, man." The young doctor stared at his blood-stained handkerchief. "What's the matter with you? Don't you feel well?"

"You hurt me."

"I slapped your face. You were talking to yourself, I tried to snap you out of whatever it was had caused it." He winced as he touched his mouth. "What happened, Curt?"

"I don't know." Suddenly all the rage seemed to drain from him, leaving him weak and ill, ashamed and defenceless. "I'm sorry, Carter. You startled me. I was thinking of an old friend."

"Comain?"

"Yes."

"I thought so. You spoke his name. Twice. Then I slapped you." Carter stared wonderingly at his hand.

"How many times did you hit me?"

"I don't know. Why?"

"I thought that I was fast, but you moved faster than any man I've ever seen. I didn't even know what was happening." He nodded to the two miners. "You can let him go now, he won't do it again."

Tiredly Curt slumped into a chair and stared at the floor. He felt ill, physically ill, and, at the same time, he was conscious of a peculiar sense of power. Something was wrong. He had thought of an old friend, dead now for more than two centuries, and suddenly it had seemed as if Comain had stood before him, smiling, talking, *real*. Then the pain of the blow and the electron-swift reaction. He had lied to Carter. He remembered his blows, five of them, all delivered within the space of…of…

He frowned. Incredible as it seemed he couldn't recall any passage of time during the incident, but it had been between the impact and the withdrawing of the young doctor's hand. And that meant he had moved fast.

A muted drone hummed in the silence of the room and light flared on a dark sheet of smooth plastic. It swirled, steadied, and a woman stared into the room.

"Doctor Lasser?"

"Yes?"

"Decision from Comain. The majority of the Martian colonists are to be transported to Everest. They will construct an observatory there. Machines for levelling the top of the mountain have already left. Transportation will be provided at dawn tomorrow for the selected personnel."

"I see." Lasser glared at the calm features of the woman. "You mentioned a 'majority'. Does that mean that some of us are to be separated from the main group?"

"Yes. Yourself and your assistants are to report to the Central Hospital. There your acquired skill can be used to the best advantage. Others will work as directed. You will receive copies of the decision within an hour. That is all."

"That is all." Lasser snarled at the darkening screen. "So I'm to be a janitor in a hospital, am I? Well, we'll see about that!"

Savagely he pressed a button beneath the screen.

"Information."

"Yes?" A smooth-faced man looked inquiringly at the angry doctor. "What can I do for you?"

"I wish to consult Comain. How do I go about it?"

"Don't you know?" Almost the man smiled. "There are public booths in every city. Find one, obey the instructions, and you may ask your question."

"Thank you." Lasser switched off the videophone and strode towards the door.

"Where are you going?" Carter stepped before the old man. "Are you crazy, Lasser? You know that they won't let you out of the building. Calm down, man. We've got to think this one out."

"Why? If that machine says that I should work in a hospital, then it can tell me how to dodge it. Anyway, I'm going to ask."

"And if it asks you to don the helmet?" Carter nodded at the sudden look of understanding in the old man's eyes. "Exactly. We've gone to a lot of trouble to keep Curt a secret. Are you going to throw all that away now?"

"No." Wearily the old man sank into a chair. "What shall we do, Carter? How can we break the stranglehold Comain has on this planet?"

"I don't know, but I do know that our only hope lies in Curt. He is the one man who can help us."

"Before I can do that I've a lot to learn." Curt rose from his chair and crossing the room stared out of the window. "You forget that I know nothing of this world. How am I going to live? Where? What shall I call myself? What shall I someone asks me for my registration number? If I'm to be of any use to you I've got to know these things."

"He's right, Lasser." Carter stared at the old man. "It's time we made some plans, and the first thing is to give Curt a number." He frowned at his own wrist with its neatly tattooed serial index.

"That's easy." Wendis bared his own wrist. "We can invent one."

"No. If they check with Comain and find that his number isn't registered, they will know at once that he is suspect. No. It would be best to give him one of ours. Better in a way, it could be a form of alibi."

"Good enough." Wendis nodded and thrust out his arm. "He can have mine."

"That's settled then. I'll copy it in indelible ink, it will be fast, but he can remove it with a chemical if necessary. Now, for the general background." Carter stared at the silent figure of the young man by the window. "You know by now that Comain rules the planet, in fact if not in name. You must always be careful to avoid registration, on no account must you ever don the helmet, and don't let anyone persuade you to either."

"I understand." Curt turned from the window. "You know," he said quietly. "All this seems just a little fantastic. You talk of a machine which can assimilate all data and predict coming events from that information. I grasp the idea, but the thing must be intricate beyond imagination. How was it ever built?"

"It wasn't," said Lasser curtly. "It grew." He nodded towards the huge building framed in the window. "That thing has been growing for two and a half centuries now. At first it was a glorified calculating machine, then a limited value predictor, now it is almost a God."

"Comain was an atheist," said Curt quietly. "He wouldn't like to be called a God."

"It isn't what the machine wants, it's what the people decide, and I tell you, Curt, they almost worship that thing."

"Perhaps, but never mind that now. How do I live?"

"I don't know," admitted Lasser, sombrely. "I'd hoped that we could all give you a part of our wages, but if we are to be separated that won't be possible. You could get a job, of course, but that may not be too easy."

"How about gambling?" Curt grinned as he asked the question. "I used to be pretty lucky with a pair of dice."

"Gambling is legal. Every city has its pleasure palace and casino, but where are you going to get money for a stake?"

"From you, of course, where else?"

Lasser nodded, and Wendis stirred impatiently from where he stood by the darkened videophone.

"We can give him what we receive from the sale of our personal possessions," he snapped. "What I want to know is what do we do after that? How are we going to wreck Comain?"

"We are not going to wreck Comain." Lasser glared at the young man. "We are going to force the Matriarch to grant us an independent Mars. The only way we can do that is to disturb things to such an extent that they will be glad to get rid of us. Any talk of rebellion or wrecking will bring the metamen after us, and you know what that means."

"Imprisonment?"

"Yes. Any attempt to sabotage Comain is punishable with five hundred years forced labour."

"What?" Curt stared at the old man. "You must be mistaken. No man can live five hundred years."

"No man has lived five hundred years," corrected Lasser, grimly. "But that is only because the metamen are relatively new." He smiled humourlessly at the young man. "You haven't met them yet have you? Wait until you do, then you will understand how a man can be forced to labour for half a millennium. Death would be a pleasure in comparison."

He spun at the sound of a heavy tread outside the door, and silently the five men waited for the portal to open.

Something entered the room.

It was tall, ten feet from the soles of its metal feet to the top of its cone-shaped head. It moved with a mechanical precision and it looked like a demented parody of a man. It thudded to a halt and from its twin scanning lenses deep ruby light flickered and pulsed.

"Doctor Lasser?" Its voice was cold, inhuman, like the sounds made by vibrating plastic and electrical current.

"Yes?" Lasser stepped forward.

"Decision of Comain." The thing raised its articulated arm and held out a thin sheaf of papers. "Take them."

Lasser took the papers from the metal hand and stood waiting while the thing turned and thudded from the room.

"What was it?" Curt wiped sweat from his face and palms. "A robot?"

"That was a metamen," said Lasser grimly. "The Matriarch probably sent it as a reminder to obey the predictions of Comain." He stared at Wendis. "Now you know why you mustn't even think of wrecking the machine. Those things are potentially immortal, and how would you like to wear that metal shell and work at forced labour for the next five hundred years?"

"Those things," whispered Curt sickly, "men?"

"The brains of men in mechanical bodies. Mostly those who have died by accident, or those who deliberately chose the potential immortality of a robot-like life to inevitable death. They are the guards of Comain, the servants of the Matriarch, emotionless, unfeeling, perfect servants and police. These are the elite of course, criminals are exiled to the Moon, but elite or not, the metamen are dangerous and will hunt a man to his death."

"I see," said Curt, and stared out of the window towards the huge building.

Suddenly he wanted very much to get out of the room.

CHAPTER XII

Night had fallen and the city of Comain glittered with ten thousand co-loured lights, the great bulk of the central building scintillating with illuminated landing stages, terraces, speckled with lighted windows and glowing with floodlit radiance. Cars droned softly along the wide roads and people, careless, casual people, sauntered between high buildings as they walked towards their evening recreation.

Curt felt his pulses leap with excitement as he moved among them.

He wore a utilitarian suit of dull grey, a combination of slacks and high collared blouse, soft and comfortable against his skin. Money rested in his pocket, the proceeds of the sale of all the Martian's personal possessions, and on his left wrist his skin tingled to the freshly applied chemical of an indelible number. Lasser had told him all he could, the old doctor knew more about conditions on Earth than any of the others, and now, with Wendis at his side, Curt was exploring the sprawling area of the Capital city.

"Any ideas, Curt?"

"Perhaps." Curt frowned as the Asteroid Miner stepped closer. Despite himself Curt didn't trust the man. He was too intense, too eager for action, too careless of his own and others' safety. Wendis was a fanatic with a one track mind, the type of man who would cheerfully destroy a city or a civilisation to achieve his own ends. Curt didn't mind that. He had no delusions as to why the Martians had smuggled him to Earth, and he knew that to the gaunt doctor and the fanatical Wendis he was but a tool, something to be used so that they could get their own way.

But sometimes a tool could use the user.

He halted before a terraced building, staring at the swirling beauty of ever-changing colour from kaleidoscopic floodlights as they bathed the smooth concrete in shimmering waves of red and blue, green and yellow, merging and weaving in an eye-catching pattern. People moved through the wide double doors a colourful, happy throng, and soft music spilled from the building.

"Well?" Wendis jerked his head towards the wide doors. "Going in?"

"Is this the casino?"

"Yes." The young miner stared contemptuously at the building. "This is where the decadent so-called men of Earth spend their recreation time.

You can get anything here, drink, drugs, gambling, anything. These pleasure palaces provide the main form of amusement now."

"Drugs?" Curt smiled. "What do you mean? Tobacco?"

"I mean what I say. Come on, the quicker we get to work the better." Impatiently Wendis thrust towards the wide doors and shrugging, Curt followed him into the huge building.

A great hall stretched before him, a smoothly finished expanse of gleaming plastic, and from it stairs and passages led to various parts of the building. Down both walls a row of cubicles, looking something like the public telephone kiosks of his own age, stretched in close array and from them, a continuous stream of people eddied and swirled. Almost all the new arrivals seemed to head for the booths, entering, staying a few moments, then either making their way to one or the other of the passages, or, in a few cases, leaving the building. Curt touched Wendis on the arm and jerked his head towards the booths.

"What are they?"

"Public consultation booths. The fools are finding out whether or not they will enjoy themselves tonight. If they get a high prediction, they stay, if not, they leave and try something else."

"You mean that if Comain tells them that they won't have a good time they believe it?"

"Naturally. Isn't that what Lasser has been telling you all along?" The young miner scowled and headed towards a flight of stairs. "Come on. Let's see if you are still lucky."

The gambling rooms occupied a whole floor of the great building and Curt stared across the brilliantly lit expanse as he tried to recognise the various machines and layouts. People thronged the room, men and women, their faces flushed with excitement, and the steady droning of the croupiers and the endless clicking of chips and coins blended into muted sound.

"What are you going to try first? The dice?"

"I don't know yet. I want to look around for a while. You forget, all this is new to me."

"Suit yourself," grunted Wendis. "I'm going to get a drink. I'll meet you over by the dice table, the third one from the end; this hanging about is getting on my nerves."

"Maybe you should go back to the hotel and let Menson act as watchdog?" Curt stared at the angry face of the young miner. "It's about time that you realised I don't like being pushed around, Wendis. I'm not your property to do as you order. I'll play in my own good time."

"Then play, or cut your throat, or go to hell for all I care. I'm fed up with this. I want to get back home to Mars, and the sooner the better."

"Will getting drunk help?"

"Damned if I know, but I'm going to try it." He hesitated, then grinned, looking surprisingly young and foolish. "Sorry, Curt, but I'm all wound up inside. See you later?"

"Yes." Curt stared after the tense figure of the miner, then shrugging, turned to examine the gambling devices which almost filled the huge room.

Something like a slot machine stood close beside him and he examined it, studying the brilliant plastic and coloured metal. A small trap at the top of the machine released a ball, the game appeared to be to decide which of two channels the ball would take. It was a simple game paying even money, and he turned from it, looking for something more in his line. Other machines flanked the walls, some incredibly complex and paying high odds, others as simple as the first and hardly worth more than a curious glance. He halted before something which reminded him of an old-fashioned pipe organ, and watched as a woman thrust coins into a slot.

Light flared behind a clear sheet of plastic and tiny motes searing of brilliance spilled from the pipes, weaving and turning in a complex rhythm. Rapidly the woman pressed a series of buttons and a web of luminescence engulfed the brilliant motes. For a moment the two lights seemed to hang suspended in invisible combat, then the web died and the motes flared in splendid victory.

Biting her lips the woman moved away, and, after watching others wage their skill, Curt moved after her. That machine was not for him.

The droning of a croupier presiding over a spinning wheel attracted his attention and he watched the players push piles of coins onto a squared board. The wheel, a treble ring of black and white compartments, spun and a flickering point of light hovered above the spinning disc. It settled, the wheel stopped, and the voice of the impassive croupier echoed in the momentary silence.

"Central white. Odds a thousand to one. Place your bets please."

Curt shrugged and moved on.

He felt restless, uneasy, tense and excited. Everything was so different, the clothes everyone wore, the casual indifference, the impression of carelessness as if no one had any cares or personal worries. It was only at the tables that he felt at home. He recognised the intent expressions, the flush of excitement and the eagerness of the gamblers as they placed their bets, but even here there was the same impression of indifference as if they knew that what they did wasn't really important.

He halted by an expanse of green baize and smiled at the sight of familiar dice as they tumbled and rolled over the smooth surface.

This was for him.

Curt pressed forward, dragging money from his pocket and watching the flow of play. A man rattled the dice, threw them, grunted at the result and turned away. Curt nodded at the croupier and dropped several notes onto the table.

"Yes?"

"Sure." Skilfully the man covered the bet and tossed the dice. Curt swept them up, feeling their smooth surfaces, rolling them between his palms. Abruptly he flung them against the end of the table.

"Eight." The croupier returned the cubes. "The point is eight."

"Here it comes." Curt rolled and threw.

"Nine. Try again." The dice bounced and settled.

"Seven. You lose."

Curt shrugged and passed over the dice. He hadn't really expected to win, not at first, and patiently he waited until the dice passed around the table.

"Ten credits. Right?"

"You're covered." Curt nodded and rolled the dice.

"Seven! A winner!"

"Let it ride."

"Seven again!"

"Let it ride." Curt licked his lips, feeling the familiar tension of a gambler on a lucky streak warming his stomach. Slowly he threw the cubes, sending them skittering across the table, bouncing them from the baffle at the far end.

"Seven again!" The croupier glanced at the young man. "Again?"

"Why not. Let it ride." Around him he could feel the silent tension of the watching crowd. Three wins in a row wasn't too unusual but it was unusual enough to arouse interest, and Curt smiled as he felt the cubes roll against his palm. He smiled, then, concentrating on throwing a seven, he threw the dice.

Again he won, and again he left the pile of money where it was. Now he stood to win a hundred and sixty credits, and if he could win again....

He did.

And again.

And again.

It almost grew monotonous. The dice bounced and spun, gleaming in the brilliant lights and falling to show the inevitable seven. Each time he won he doubled his money, and around him, swelling like a dammed river, the tension of the watching crowd grew to a high-pitched excitement.

"He can't keep on winning," said a woman. "I'll bet a thousand against him this throw."

"What odds?"

"Five to one."

"I'll take it," said a man, and chuckled as he saw another winning seven. "Want to bet again?"

"He can't keep on winning!" There was a note of desperation in the woman's voice. "Another thousand."

"Same odds?"

"Yes."

Curt thinned his lips as he rolled the dice. So he couldn't keep on winning? Well, he would see about that. Grimly he concentrated on the spinning cubes, willing them to show a seven. They slowed, toppled, seemed to hesitate, then, with a final jerk, settled on the green cloth.

"It can't be true!" Frantic disbelief echoed in the worn voice. "Another seven! It just isn't possible!"

"You owe me a thousand," reminded the man calmly. "Want to bet again?"

"No. I haven't any more money. Comain predicted that I wouldn't lose tonight. Now I've lost. I can't understand it!"

"You want to throw again, sir?" The croupier stared at Curt.

"Yes."

"You've reached the limit for this table. I can't cover your bet."

"Can't you?" Curt shrugged and picked up the thick pile credit notes. "I'll pull out then. Here." Casually he threw the dice, not thinking about them, not caring. They spun, seeming to wink in the bright lighting.

Snake eyes.

Casually Curt moved from the table and sauntered across the room. He avoided the modernised roulette table, the mock battle game and the unfamiliar electronic devices. He found what he was looking for in a corner of the vast room, and stood, smiling down at the familiar red and black lay-out of an old-fashioned roulette wheel.

Casually he placed a bet, and lost. He bet again, watching the spinning ball settle into its compartment, and smiled as the croupier raked in his money. Again he bet, and this time concentrated on the tiny ball, willing it as he had done the dice, concentrating his thoughts and fixing a colour in his mind.

"Twenty black." The little rake collected the bets and pushed out the winnings, and Curt stared at the little heap of money lying on the cloth before him. Again he narrowed his eyes as he concentrated on the leaping ball, and again it clicked into a black compartment. The heap of money grew higher, and Curt became conscious of a mounting excitement.

This was no ordinary gambler's lucky streak. He was lucky, he had always known that, but never before had he been as lucky as this. He remembered the dice and how he had willed them to fall on winning numbers. He thought of the leaping ball of the roulette wheel, and how he had lost until he concentrated on it. And now…

It almost seemed as if he could control the spinning ball.

He experimented. He bet on colours, on numbers, narrowing his eyes and willing the ball to register the number he desired. He won. He kept on winning. He won until it became monotonous and before him the heaped pile of credit notes grew and grew as the sweating croupier wielded his little rake.

And around him grew a watching crowd.

They followed his bets that crowd. They waited for him to place his money, and then poured their wealth upon the marked cloth. As he won, they won, and flushed faces and mounting tension ringed the table and the spinning wheel. Curt felt irritated at their presence, his nerves crawling to the flux of their avid emotion, and deliberately he began to lose, hoping that the watchers would leave him alone.

"Ten thousand on the red."

The wheel spun, the tiny ball flickered around the compartmented rim, and the croupier gasped with relief as he stared down at the winning number.

"Zero. Black." His hands trembled a little as he cleared the board. "Place your bets."

"Ten thousand on the red." Curt smiled as he looked at the spinning wheel, and smiled again at the disappointed sighs from the crowd. "Ten thousand on the red."

Again he lost, and again, and yet again. Behind him a woman muttered disgustedly as she moved from the table, and a man cursed as he saw the last of his wealth drawn beneath the croupier's rake.

"The streak's over. He can't win again tonight."

"I'm going to consult Comain. I was predicted a good night and I feel as miserable as hell. Broke too."

"Let's try something else. There's a hoodoo on this table."

"To hell with him. He's cost me plenty."

Curt grinned as he heard the various comments from the disgusted crowd, and continued to lose at every spin of the wheel. The croupier regained his calm as he saw the heap of notes dwindling and flowing to his side of the table, and his voice resumed its emotionless drone.

"Place your bets. No more play."

The wheel spun and Curt lost.

"Place your bets."

"Winning?" Wendis leaned over the table and Curt could smell the sickly sweet odour of exotic liqueurs on the young man's breath. "How's it going, Curt? Made enough to retire on yet?"

"No."

"I thought so." Wendis swayed and caught at the edge of the table to steady himself. "You can't win on these tables. No one can win. We don't stand a chance."

"Think not?"

"I know not. The damn thing's fixed like everything else on this rotten planet. The machine won't let you win. It won't let you do anything."

"You hate Comain don't you, Wendis?" Curt stared at the spinning wheel. "Why?"

"You ask me that?" Anger steadied the young man and he straightened, glaring at Curt. "Do you think I like being ruled by a collection of wires and tubes? Of course I hate Comain. Who wouldn't? It's only these gutless swine who are content to live in their safe, snug little world. I'm not like them. I'm a man, and I want to live as a man should."

"So you want to blow up the machine, ruin a civilisation, reduce Earth to anarchy and to civil war."

"Why not? I'm not interested in Earth. I'm only interested in Mars."

"Would money get you there?"

"What?" Wendis licked his lips as he tried to think clearly through the mists of alcohol. "What are you talking about?"

"If you had money, a lot of money, would that satisfy you? Could you buy a space ship, stores, arrange supplies? If you had wealth would the Matriarch permit you to use it to reestablish the Martian colony?"

"I don't know," said Wendis slowly. "I've never thought about it. Yes. I suppose that it could be done. They only forced us to return because we were dependent on Earth for supplies. If we could have brought our own we'd never have come back."

"Very well then," said Curt quietly. "I'll get you money, a lot of money, and after that I want you to leave me alone."

Abruptly he thrust what remained of the pile of notes onto the table. "The lot, on double zero."

"Yes, sir." The croupier smiled as he spun the wheel, and Curt narrowed his eyes as he stared at the dancing ball. Within his skull his brain seemed to be made of fire, burning and vibrant with rushing blood and crystal clear thought. Little tremors quivered his nerves and he felt his palms grow wet with perspiration.

The wheel slowed and the ball clicked into a compartment.

"Double Zero!" The croupier stared unbelievingly at the halted wheel. "You win."

"Leave it," snapped Curt. "Spin again."

"Yes, sir." The man sighed with relief as he spun the wheel. "As you wish, sir." He stood, leaning against the edge of the table, and waited impatiently for the wheel to stop. The young man was a fool. It was against all possibility that he could win on the same number twice running. The odds against it were too high and the money was as good as back in the bank. Sweat started to his forehead as he stared at the tiny white ball in its compartment, and his voice was a croak as he announced winning number.

"Double Zero!"

"Let it ride." Curt smiled as he looked at Wendis. "So the wheel is fixed, is it? A man can't win, you said. Well? What am I doing now?"

"Double Zero!" The croupier sounded ill.

"Let it ride."

"Double Zero!"

"Let it ride."

The pile of money mounted, spilling over the table and falling to the floor. Wendis stared at it, his eyes clearing and his breath quickening as he watched the croupier mechanically thrusting more money to the mounting pile.

"Curt! What's happening here?"

"Place your bets," whispered the croupier sickly.

"Let it ride." Curt stared at the young miner. "Do you think that will be enough?"

"I don't know. How much have you won?"

Curt shrugged, staring at the spinning wheel. It stopped, tiny ball clicking into its compartment.

"Double Zero!" The croupier dropped his rake. "Again! You've won every time. I can't understand it."

"Spin your wheel," snapped Curt.

"I can't. You've broken the bank. There's no more money."

"What? Impossible. This table hasn't got a bank. There's no limit." Wendis glared at the pale-faced croupier. "Spin that wheel!"

"Hold it, Wendis." Curt stared at the pile of money. "There's enough here for what you want."

"What I want? You mean that you're giving it all to me?"

"Not all." Curt stuffed some of the money into his pockets. "You can have the rest, you and the colonists." He look the croupier. "How much have I won?"

"More than any other man in history," whispered the croupier. "All the money in the room. Twenty million credits!"

He stared sickly at the great heap of credit notes littering the marked cloth on the table.

CHAPTER XIII

Nyeeda sat at her desk and conducted the normal business of the day. As usual she wore iridescent black and the late afternoon sun reflected from a wide band of intricately fashioned gold around her left wrist. Her secretary, a plainly dressed, middle-aged woman, worked quietly at her desk and aside from the soft sounds of her keyboard, silence filled the office.

A videophone chimed its muted warning and the screen flared with swirling brilliance.

"Yes?"

"Report from the Trans-European Stratolines, Madam. They state that one of their passenger transports is overdue at the airport. The flight had a three nines favourable prediction."

"Then the ship will arrive," said Nyeeda flatly. "Three nines is a high probability. Nothing can have happened to the stratoliner."

"As you say, Madam." The woman pictured in the screen hesitated and glanced at something in her hand. "Further reports. Three cases of unpredicted accidents in the city. The reclamation squads arrival too late to save the brains, and death was final. Five cases of complaint that high probability predictions did not materialise. One request from the owners of the casino for consultation with Comain on the restricted level."

"What?" Nyeeda frowned as she stared at the screen. "For what reason?"

"The prediction of profit has proved utterly wrong. The casino was almost bankrupt last night."

"What of it? Don't they know that it is impossible for Comain to predict anything depending on utter chance?"

"Yes, Madam, but they request a personal interview with the Matriarch."

"I will attend to them. Anything else?"

"No, I…" The woman paused as someone outside the range of the scanners attracted her attention. "Fresh news on the stratoliner, Madam. Wreckage has been sighted fifty miles out to sea. Examination proves that it must have come from the missing ship."

"What!" Nyeeda swallowed and the middle-aged woman sitting at her desk paused in her work and stared at the young secretary. "I will attend to it," snapped Nyeeda. "Inform me of any fresh developments."

"Yes Madam." The screen blurred and went dark.

For a long moment Nyeeda sat motionless at her desk and, when at last she moved, it was with a grim determination. "I am going to consult Comain," she snapped at her secretary. "Then I shall visit the Matriach. Record anything of importance."

The middle-aged woman nodded and resumed her typing.

An elevator carried Nyeeda deep into the heart of the building and she left the cage at a point three hundred feet below sea level. A metaman, its scanning eyes flaring with ruby light, stepped before her, then, as she gave the password, stood aside and let her pass. A short passage opened onto a wide area, and crossing it, the girl pressed her palm against a sensitised plate sunken into the wall beside the thin slit of a closed door. Machinery hummed as the lines of her palm registered on the plate, and, the pattern tripping the electronic relays, the door slid smoothly to one side, exposing a small chamber.

Within that chamber waited Comain.

A chair, a low shelf, a scanning eye and speaker, a microphone and a helmet of some dull metal. That was Comain. Not the machine of course. Not the ranks of memory banks and the intricate miles of wire, the compact atomic piles and the millions of electronic tubes, these were hidden far below, but, nonetheless, this was Comain.

Nyeeda sat on the chair and stared at the scanning eye. A switch moved beneath her fingers and a cold, utterly inhuman voice echoed from the speaker.

"Yes?"

"Nyeeda, secretary to the Matriarch, accredited and authorised to use restricted level." She pressed her bared left wrist against the scanning eye as she spoke the routine identification.

"Yes?"

"A passenger transport of Trans-European Stratolines has been wrecked. The flight had a favourable prediction of three nines. Why did it crash?"

"Insufficient data. Don the helmet."

Obediently Nyeeda rested the dull helmet over her long black hair. A red lamp flashed on the panel and she removed it, waiting patiently for the machine to speak.

"The unknown factor," droned the speaker. "Three nines is not certainty."

"It is as near to it as to make no difference. This is the first time such a thing has happened. Explain."

"No accident was predicted. No accident should have taken place."

"It did."

"The unknown factor."

"I see." Nyeeda bit her lip. "What of the other things?"

"Three unpredictable accidents show the influence of some unregistered force. All predictions must be suspect until full data is given."

"Full data has been given," snapped the girl. "With the registering of the Martian colonists every person on the planet has given his or her information to the memory banks. How can there be an unregistered force?"

"There is such a force."

"I see." Nyeeda frowned at the blank wall of the cubicle. As usual when consulting Comain she had an almost overwhelming impression that she spoke to a living person instead of what was no more than an elaborate machine. Long ago the typed symbols of the original predictor had been replaced by verbal and aural communication and the inevitable result was that people tended more and more to regard the machine as something intelligent and alive. It wasn't, of course, the responses came from the memory banks, were translated into words, and echoed from the speaker, but the impression remained and it was hard not to think of Comain as a man.

"Predict the time of discovering this unknown force."

"A paradoxical question. As the force is unknown it is impossible to predict its date of discovery. If such a prediction could be made the force would not be unknown."

"I see." Nyeeda stared at the ruby fight of the scanning eye. "What of the casino?"

"No prediction is possible for the so-called law of averages. It is just as likely for a coin to fall heads a million times as it is for it to fall either way each time."

"But you didn't predict that the casino would be almost bankrupt."

"Unknown factor."

"Explain."

"Prediction was based on known data. Knowledge of persons involved precluded any one of them continuing to gamble after reaching a certain figure. Normal win and loss of the casino would have evened out. Some force disturbed that prediction."

"The same force that caused three unpredicted accidents and wrecked a stratoliner?"

"Prediction of unknown factor nine nines probability."

"Is it a man?"

"Insufficient data."

"It can't be a man." Nyeeda stared helplessly at the panel of the machine. "We know that every man and woman on Earth has registered, and yet you say that there is an unknown factor. Can you give a date for the beginning of this unknown force?"

"No such force detected before the landing of the Martian colonists."

"So they are to blame." Anger flushed the secretary's white cheeks. "They have caused nothing but trouble, but we'll stop it now. I'll see that they all re-register, that should clear up this mystery." She hesitated, looking at the machine, conscious as she always was of the questions which could be asked if only she dared to hear the answer.

She could find out the date of the Matriarch's death. She could find out whether or not she would succeed to the Matriarchy. She could even find out the date of her own death.

If she dared to know the answer.

She didn't. She knew it, knew too that if she did ask the knowledge of her question would be recorded in the machine and others could find out what she had done. Slowly she left the cubicle, the door sliding shut behind her. The metaman stared at her as she passed and the elevator carried her back to the top of the building.

When she arrived the Matriarch was waiting.

"Well?" The old woman thinned her lips as she stared at her secretary. "Did Comain give you all the answers?"

"No, Madam. All I could learn was that an unknown force is operating to render all predictions inaccurate. The force commenced with the landing of the Martian colonists and must be connected with them in some way."

"I could have told you that myself." The Matriarch snorted as she rustled among her papers. "I consulted Comain as soon as I learned of what happened at the casino last night."

"What are we to do, Madam? If Comain can't help us..." Nyeeda looked helplessly at the old woman.

"Then we must help ourselves. Now. I have interviewed the croupier who operated the roulette wheel which lost all that money. He has described the person who won, and, naturally, has given that information to Comain. It is a man, an unregistered man. There can be no doubt of it."

"Unregistered?" Nyeeda stared her surprise. "How can that be?"

"Why ask me? You were in charge of the landing. Obviously the man came from Mars."

"No. The man couldn't have been a colonist. The metamen counted them, registered them, and besides, if he had been, Comain would have known of him."

"That is true." The Matriarch frowned as she pondered the question. "Yet this unknown force is a man. Comain did not recognise him from the memories of the croupier so we must assume that he is unregistered. Whoever he is he won twenty million credits last night, caused three unpredicted accidents, and has given us more trouble with the Martians."

"How so?"

"They want to buy a space ship. They want to buy supplies and equipment. They want to go back to Mars."

"Then why not let them?"

"Are you a fool, Nyeeda? Why do you think we brought them to Earth in the first place? It was to have them beneath our full control. We forced them back, and they came because they were dependant on us for supplies. Now they have money, a lot of money, and they seem to think that they can get more. Now do you see the problem?"

"Refuse them a space ship. Bar them from leaving."

"And cause dissension?" The old woman shook her head. "Once we start doing that, Nyeeda, we won't know where to stop. No. A man or woman must have the right to spend their own money in their own way. We daren't tamper with that right. All we can do is to cause delay, I've already done that, and hope that after a while they will be content to remain here." She gritted her teeth. "The main thing is to get hold of this unregistered man. Nothing can be done until then."

"Is he so important?" Nyeeda shrugged as she picked up the reproduced likeness of what the man probably looked like. "He seems very young. Is he so dangerous?"

"Dangerous! That man threatens the entire safety of our civilisation!" The Matriarch slumped in her chair. "Years ago it wouldn't have mattered so much, but now, now that we are so dependent on Comain, he is the most dangerous thing which could happen to us. Think of it, Nyeeda. Everything he does, every action he takes, disturbs the predictions on which our civilisation is built. Last night he won twenty million credits. The mere fact of him doing that altered the predictions of three people. Perhaps they stayed longer than they would have done, watching him play. Perhaps they met him, spoke to him, did something, anything which caused them to be at a certain place at a certain time. A place and time when normally they would have been out of harm's way. Perhaps the pilot of that stratoliner was thinking about him when the ship crashed. Perhaps anything, but we must get that man, Nyeeda, and get him soon."

"The metamen?"

"They have been alerted. His likeness will be displayed in every public place and a reward of a million credits offered for his capture."

"But won't that do the very thing you fear most? All these unpredicted actions will make it necessary for Comain to revise every scrap of data."

"What of it? If we don't do it he will upset everything anyway. If we do, and it is as good as done by now, then we will get some information to work on. Once we know where he is, how he reacts to danger, where he is likely to go, then Comain can predict his future actions and make capture simple. But we must know more about him."

"One man," said Nyeeda slowly. "It seems incredible that one extra man should make all this difference."

"It was a danger we couldn't foresee. Every birth and death is registered. How the devil he managed to escape registration I don't know." The old woman frowned down at her fingers. "We can find all that out later. Now we must get this man. Hunt him down like a dog. Kill him if necessary, but get him, and get him soon."

"Am I in charge of the search?"

"Yes."

"Very well, Madam. I'll have him for you within two days."

"You'd better," said the Matriarch grimly, and Nyeeda shuddered to her unspoken threat.

CHAPTER XIV

The park was an oasis of calm in a city of bustling strife. Lawns, smooth and green in the late afternoon sun, stretched between flowering shrubs and soaring trees. Flowers filled the air with a heady fragrance and birds trilled and chirped in the leafy branches. Little paths wound between the lawns and seats, comfortable benches of weatherproof plastic rested in quiet places.

Curt Rosslyn sat on one and relaxed in the summer warmth.

It was time for him to think things out. So far he had rode with the tide, did as he was told, believed what others wanted him to believe. So far he had had little choice. His awakening on Mars, the journey to Earth, the rush and excitement of contact with a, to him, new civilisation, had prevented him from clear thought. Now he was free of all that. Free from Wendis and Lasser, from Carter and Menson. Free of their propaganda and their selfish interests. Last night he had dodged away from the casino and wandered the streets for hours before finding this park. Since then he had slept a little and thought a lot.

First. What was it about him which could determine the fall of a pair of dice or the dropping of a tiny ball into a selected compartment? He had never been able to do it before, though, like most gamblers, he had found that concentration helped him to win. But this was more than that.

A leaf rested on the path before him, a tiny scrap of green against the old ivory of the concrete. He stared at it, concentrating his thoughts, keening the edge of his mind.

The leaf moved.

It rose a fraction and fluttered. It shifted and spun as if there were a wind, but the trees remained silent and their branches did not rustle to the slightest of breezes. There was no wind. Again he concentrated, feeling his brain burn within his skull and the cold sweat of nervous exhaustion started to his forehead. Again the leaf moved, tilted, and suddenly darted away.

Telekinesis!

Curt knew about it, had read about it and even wondered whether such things as paraphysical phenomena could ever exist. Now he had proved that it could. The only logical explanation for what had happened was that he had controlled the movements of dice and ball, of wheel and leaf with the power of his own mind. He had willed them to move—and they had moved. Somehow, something, had changed him from a normal into…

Into what?

He shrugged, shelving the problem. What he was and how he had turned from a normal man into someone who could control unusual powers was something which could wait. Now he had to decide what to do.

Despite what Lasser and the others had told him he had little sympathy for the Martians. They had revived him and for that he was grateful, but he had given them twenty million credits and considered the debt wiped out. They had a grudge, that was natural, but he could also see the problem from the other side. It was uneconomical to pour wealth into a colony which could not survive. Also, if Lasser had spoken the truth, it was not just a matter of keeping a few hundred people on an arid planet. The future of this civilisation depended on their presence on Earth.

Comain wanted them back home.

He smiled as he remembered his friend. It was hard to remember that the man and the machine weren't the same thing. It had seemed such a little time ago that he had heard the thin man's voice over the radio, that they had stood together on the wastes of Poker Flats and stared up at the distant stars as they dreamed their individual dreams.

He missed Comain.

Now? Now he had to fend for himself. One man couldn't break an established system of government. No matter what Lasser had said Curt knew that. And really the problem was a simple one. He had to choose between a lost Mars and a real Earth. Earth! He smiled as he stared at the trees and flowers. A wife perhaps, children, a comfortable old age. All the things he had thought lost forever. His now. Waiting for him as soon as he could fit in this new and interesting world.

Slowly he rose from the bench and walked from the park.

The booth looked so much like a telephone kiosk that he almost passed it before he realised that it was the thing he was looking for. He entered, closing the door behind him and feeling a peculiar stir of excitement deep in his stomach as he stared at the dull helmet, the ruby scanning eye, the chair and the low shelf.

Comain!

Nervously he sat down and pressed the signal button.

"Yes?"

"Information, please."

"Your name and serial number?"

"Wendis. Number…" He began to read it aloud when he was interrupted.

"Place your bared wrist against the scanning eye."

"Yes. As you wish." Nervously he rested his wrist against the smooth face of the red-lit eye. "That right?"

"Yes!"

"Good."

Silence as he stared at the blank panel of the machine and he shifted uncomfortably in his seat as he waited for the machine to speak. It didn't, and with a start he realised that he had lifted his finger from the activating button. Grimly he pressed it.

"Yes?"

"Information, please."

"Identify yourself."

"Wendis." Curt remembered and rested his left wrist against the scanning eye.

"Yes?"

Curt nervously licked his dry lips, remembering to keep his finger hard against the button and wishing that he had asked as to the correct procedure of consulting Comain.

"What is the penalty for not registering?"

"Ten years forced labour."

"I see. How does a man register?"

"Don the helmet."

"That all?"

"Yes."

Curt shivered, the cold, inhuman tones from the speaker making him wish that he had never entered the booth. For a moment he struggled with the desire to get up and leave the booth with its inhuman voice and unfamiliar controls. Then he remembered that it was only a machine.

"What is the best way for a man to earn a living in this world?"

"Insufficient data."

"What do you mean?"

"Insufficient data."

"Damn it!" Curt glared at the scanning eye. He was beginning to realise that a machine which could answer every question had its limitations. It was only a machine. It lacked volition and could only answer the questions put to it. Answer them in a coldly logical way without adding anything to the bare answer, and not, as a man would do, filling in the unspoken questions, adding suggestions and volunteering information.

"I am a stranger in this city," said Curt slowly. "What is the best thing for me to do?"

"Don the helmet."

"What?" Curt shook his head. "I can't."

Silence as the machine waited for his next question.

"Predict my future actions." Curt grinned as he remembered what Lasser had told him. "What employment shall I do tomorrow?"

"None."

"Why not?"

"Prediction as to activities. Forty-five percent probability. Trying to buy space ship."

"What?" Curt almost released his pressure on the button as he stared at the scanning eye, then, understanding, he lifted his finger and sagged in the chair. The prediction was right—for Wendis. The machine had taken him to be the Asteroid Miner and that was just what the young man would be trying to do.

Tiredly Curt left the booth and wandered out along the street. He felt hungry, and looked around for a restaurant. He would eat, and then find a policeman and give himself up. The machine couldn't help him and he had no desire to wander the city like an outcast. Not even his ability to win money would compensate him for a total lack of companionship and understanding.

He could always win money.

The bright fights of a restaurant showed clear against the sunlight and he entered, slumping in a chair, and staring dully at a row of buttons to his right. He pressed several of them, then waited, wondering what was the next thing to do. Machinery whined beneath the smooth surface of the table, a panel slid aside, and a tray, loaded with steaming dishes, rose before him. As he lifted the tray the panel closed again and he smiled as he recognised an old idea in its modern form.

He had chosen a self-service cafeteria.

The food warmed him, easing some of the cold fear that had gripped his stomach, and he relaxed staring curiously around the crowded restaurant. At the next table a man and a woman sat, more engrossed in each other than in their food, and he noted the unabashed way in which they displayed their affection. In one way at least the world hadn't changed.

Against one wall a wide sheet of clear material suddenly flared with light and swirling colour. It steadied and a woman stared from the screen. A woman with long dark hair and eyes that were like twin pools of midnight beneath her heavy brows. She wore a dress of some shining black material and her full were red lips against the whiteness of her skin. Curt stared at her, savouring her remarkable beauty, and was barely conscious of the hush which settled over the restaurant.

"An important announcement from the Matriarch," said the woman. "Today it has been discovered that an enemy of the state is at large. This man threatens the safety of each of us, and, so important does the Matriarch consider him, that a reward of one million credits will be paid to the person giving information leading to his capture. Remember. It is vitally important that this man be captured as soon as possible. His likeness will be thrown on every public screen and will remain until such time as the Matriarch sees fit to remove it. That is all."

Her image shifted and dissolved in a writhing mass of colour, then, replacing the calm features of the woman, another likeness took shape.

Curt stared at it, feeling the blood pound through his temples and an invisible hand begin to constrict his heart. There, on the screen, drawn with remarkable clarity, was his own picture.

He heard the muted hum of conversation rise around him, the droning of many voices and the tiny sounds made by people eating. He ignored them. All he could see was the brilliant picture. His own face, subtly different in minor details, but wholly recognisable. He stared at it, and at the caption beneath the portrait.

ONE MILLION CREDITS REWARD FOR THE CAPTURE OF THIS MAN!

Numbly he rose and made his way to the exit, expecting a challenge at any moment. A woman smiled at him as he neared the door and he felt panic rise within him.

"Your bill, sir."

"Yes, of course." He dropped a wad of crumpled notes into her hand and thrust past her. Three steps from the wide portal he heard her startled exclamation.

"That man! Stop that man!"

The rest was lost in a blur of motion.

A man lunged towards him and reeled back with a pulped mouth. Another thrust out his leg and screamed with pain as Curt kicked at the extended limb. Then he was at the door and his legs thrust at the smooth concrete as he flung himself away from the restaurant.

Men stared at him. A woman screamed a warning. Something loomed from an alcove, something huge and metallic, with articulated arms and heavy metal feet. Curt skidded to a halt, staring wildly at the advancing figure of the metaman, and darted to one side.

Blue fire streamed through the air where he had stood a moment before. It swung, lifted, and Curt felt his legs go numb and almost lifeless as the blue ray stabbed past him, missing him by a fraction.

Desperately he darted between a couple of women, flung himself around a corner, and raced for the remembered sanctuary of the little park.

He didn't stand a chance. He knew that. Knew that as a stranger in a strange city they were bound to catch him within a few hours, but instinct forced him to keep running, to keep his legs thrusting against the concrete as he flung himself away from the robot-like thing pursuing him. Again the blue ray sent coldness through him, slowing his reflexes and chilling his blood with the touch of paralysis, and he sobbed with pain as he forced his sluggish muscles to carry his sagging weight.

A car droned past with a shrilling whine from its turbine. A man stared at him from the driving seat, and, with shocking abruptness, the car whined to a halt and the man tumbled out onto the roadway. He crouched, something metallic gleaming in his hand, and from his open mouth words poured in a rapid stream.

"This way. Curt! Get in the car."

"Wendis!"

"Curt, do as I say." Anger drew the young man's lips hard against his teeth. He lifted the gleaming thing in his hand and the thin, spiteful sound of shots echoed from the surrounding buildings. "Get in the car. Hurry!"

Curt grunted, throwing himself towards the open door of the low-slung turbine car, and behind him he heard Wendis curse as he fired his weapon.

Then blue fire seared him with a freezing cold and he fell into a bottomless pit of overwhelming darkness.

CHAPTER XV

Pain, and the grunted sounds made by men engaged in arduous labour. Pain, and the dull ache of heavy blows. Pain, and the screaming protest of numbed nerve and muscle as it warmed and crawled a reluctant path back to fife and awareness. Curt groaned and writhed against the grasp of many hands. He shuddered, writhed, and screamed with the searing agony of returning circulation.

As if from a great distance he heard a familiar voice.

"Steady, Curt. This is going to hurt."

It did. It filled his veins with acid and rasped his raw nerves with emery cloth. It took every cell and atom of his body and wrenched with red hot pliers. It probed deep into his brain and vibrated within the marrow of his bones. It was hell.

Blackness came then, the sweet, doubly welcome blackness of oblivion and approaching death. He sank into it, gratefully, eagerly, yielding to it as an escape from the obscene torment of physical pain. He sank, then, slowly, reluctantly, something dragged him back and lifted him into the ebbing tides of pain almost too great to bear.

Lasser stared at him with his sunken eyes.

"Take it easy, Curt. You're going to be alright now."

"What happened?" Curt licked his lips as he recognise the croaking sound as having come from his own throat. He lifted his hands and stared curiously at his trembling fingers. He touched his face and winced as pain flowed from his bruised flesh.

"The metaman got you with a para-beam. Wendis was lucky, he managed to smash the thing's scanning eyes, and got you away from the crowd. We've been working on you ever since."

"Working on me!" Curt shuddered as he dragged his protesting body to an upright position. "What were you doing, taking me apart?"

"No. You were paralysed. We had to give you artificial respiration, massage your heart, keep your blood circulating, and make sure that the brain cells didn't deteriorate. If we hadn't been lucky you'd have died for a second time—and this time it would have been for good."

"But…?" Curt grunted as he eased himself to a more comfortable position. "I'd always thought that a paralysis beam would merely knock a man down, prevent him moving his arms and legs. In my time it was considered the peace weapon of the future."

"Peace weapon." Lasser snorted contemptuously. "I suppose you thought that the voluntary muscles could be isolated and paralysed without harm to the rest of the organism? Well they can't. The para-beam can cripple a man, bring him down and render him helpless, but it is a dangerous thing to use. The heart stops. The lungs cease working, the blood stops circulating, the entire muscular system is numbed and rendered useless. The same thing happens as it does with curare. With luck and quick action it is possible to keep a man alive by artificial means until the paralysis wears off, but it is touch and go. If I hadn't been here when Wendis brought you in you'd be dead by now."

"So they meant to kill me." Curt shuddered. "Why? What harm have I done to them?"

"Isn't that obvious? You've upset the predictions of Comain. That alone would be cause enough for the Matriarch to order your death, but you've done more than that."

"Yes?"

"By winning all that money you have made us independent. Now we don't have to work on Everest. We can remain together as a unit, and while we can do that we are a continual source of irritation to the government."

"But isn't that what you wanted?"

"Perhaps." Lasser stared thoughtfully out of a window. "I'll admit that I had some such idea, but now it doesn't matter. They know about you. They know just what you look like and I'll bet that they know just how you got here. You're no longer a secret force operating against the State. You are dangerous, known, and suspect. It can only be a matter of time before you are caught."

"I see." Curt didn't trouble to hide his bitterness. "In words I've served my purpose." He rose from the narrow bunk. "I can take a hint, Lasser. I suppose that I must thank you for saving my life, but twenty million can pay off an awful lot of debts. Shall we call it square?"

"What are you talking about?"

"You don't want me any more, do you? I'm dangerous you said, and you may be right, but it doesn't really matter If you're caught hiding me you and all the colonists will trouble. I wouldn't like that." He grinned, a tight smile out humour. "Well? What are you waiting for? There is another million you can earn while you've got the chance. Why not do it?"

"I don't know what you mean." Lasser stared at the old man, but something in his sunken eyes told Curt that he had read the old man's thoughts correctly. "You don't imagine that we would turn you over to the metamen do you?"

"No? Why not? If you did you would be in the clear. Go ahead. I won't stop you."

"I…" The old man licked his lips and his sallow cheeks flushed with shame and embarrassment. "You can see how it is, Curt," he pleaded. "Things are bad enough for us as it is. If they were to find you here…" He let his voice trail into silence and stared uncomfortably at the soft carpet on the floor.

"Forget it." Curt shrugged and turned away from the old doctor. He didn't hate the old man. He didn't feel betrayed or robbed, or thrown aside. He was too old for such idealistic emotions, but at the same time he wished that Lasser hadn't made it so obvious. Now, more than ever, he felt an outcast, a stranger, unwanted by both friends and enemies. Suddenly he felt terribly alone.

The door jerked open just before he reached it and a man staggered into the room.

"Lasser. They've got Carter, Menson too!"

"Wendis!" The old man grabbed at the man and glared into his eyes. "What's happened?"

"We had gone down to the ship yards, trying to buy a space ship, and suddenly the metamen were all around us. I managed to get away, smashed the scanning eyes of two of them, and ran for the car." He gulped air and stared around the room. "Where's Curt? We've got to get him away from here."

"Why?" Curt slammed the door and faced the young miner. "What's been happening?"

"You remember when I saved you from the metaman?"

Curt nodded. "What happened then anyway? I've not had a chance to catch up since I left you last night."

"You shouldn't have done that, Curt. You should have stayed with me."

"Perhaps. But what happened?"

"After I got the money back here I bought a car and went looking for you. We all did. I was the lucky one, I spotted you as you left the restaurant and you know what happened then. After I brought you back here I found the others and we went to the ship yards. I felt that the quicker we bought a space ship the better. Anyway, while we were down there the metamen jumped us. I don't know why. Now they've got Carter and Menson and you know what that means."

"They'll be registered with Comain and the Matriarch will know all about me." Curt shrugged. "So what?"

"Are you serious?" Wendis stared his amazement. "That is the one thing we want to avoid. At all costs we must keep you in the dark until you've had a chance to wreck Comain."

"You're too late, Wendis," said Curt quietly. "I've just learned that I'm no longer wanted. In fact the quicker I get out of here and give myself up the better."

"No!"

"Yes. Ask Lasser."

"Is that true?" Wendis glared at the old man. "Did you tell him that?"

"Not exactly, but what he says makes good sense. He is dangerous to us now, Wendis. If we continue to hide him we'll all be in trouble. Comain knows of him now, his picture is spread all over town, and he can't help us any more."

"To hell with that. He's still unregistered. He can still stir things up enough to make the Matriarch wish that she had never brought us back from Mars."

"He's too dangerous," insisted the old man stubbornly. "If the metamen have caught Carter and Menson it must mean that they are after all of us. If Rosslyn is found here it means trouble."

"What of it? We can handle those things if they come for us."

"No, Wendis, we can't and you know it. Besides, you know the penalty if they catch us. Do you want to be turned into a robot?"

"Of course not."

Lasser shrugged and stared at the carpet, avoiding the young man's angry eyes.

"I know what to do," said Curt bitterly. "Let me get out of here before someone gets hurt. I wouldn't like that." He stretched his hand towards the door.

"No!" Wendis pushed Curt back into the room. "To hell with all that kind of talk. Damn it, Lasser, we can't send him out there like this. We owe him too much and it's our fault that the metamen are after him. What kind of men are we anyway? What if the robots do come? What if the whole damn Matriarchy comes? We're fighters aren't we? Well then, let's fight!"

"Are you insane, Wendis? What chance would we have?" Lasser's seamed features glistened with sweat.

"Plenty." The young Asteroid Miner thinned his lips in a tiger-snarl. Curt wasn't the only thing we smuggled from Mars. I brought a few high velocity pistols along too. I had a feeling that they might come in handy and I was right. They won't kill the metamen but the slugs can smash their scanning eyes and blind the devils. Here."

From beneath his blouse he took a glistening pistol and threw it towards Curt.

"Take it. It carries fifty slugs and each of them will kill a man with hydrostatic shock no matter where you hit. If the metamen come, aim for the scanning eyes." He stared at the old man. "Do you want one, Lasser?"

"No."

"Why not? Getting yellow?"

"Killing people won't get us back to Mars. Fighting will only earn us trouble and plenty of grief. I'm thinking of the others, Wendis, the other five hundred and seventy people who rely on us to get them back home again. What you intend doing is criminal. You have no right to risk everything for the sake of a fanatical whim."

"So standing by a friend is foolish is it?" Wendis sneered and the pistol in his hand reflected little shimmers of light as he unconsciously aimed it at the old man. "You're getting old, Lasser. You believe in talk and the nice way of doing things. Nothing wrong with that of course—except that it doesn't get us anywhere. Unless we stand up for ourselves now we're sunk, all of us, and the Matriarch will do with us as she wills. No, Lasser. I've listened to your kind of logic for too long. If the people had listened to me we'd still be on Mars and to hell with Earth, with Comain and the whole rotten mess."

"You think stopping a few metamen will get us back home?"

"Perhaps. One thing I do know. I can't throw in my hand without a struggle. I can't desert a friend when he needs me most. Right or wrong I stand by Rosslyn, and if you were half the man I thought you were you'd stand by him too."

"You fool, Wendis. You think that I like doing this?" Lasser wiped his steaming forehead. "But what else can I do? You know that we haven't a ghost of a chance to save him. He knows that himself. If we try to do the impossible we'll all wind up in a penal colony. What is the life of one man compared to hundreds? I'm not thinking of him, Wendis, because I'm thinking of Mars. I'm always thinking of Mars, and I'll do anything to get us all back there."

"He's right, Wendis." Curt smiled and held out the gun. "Here. Take it—and thanks."

"You mean it?"

"I mean it."

Wendis hesitated, staring at the outstretched pistol, and his eyes were bitter as he slowly reached for the gun.

"I think that you're making a mistake," he said. "I…" He paused, his head tilted a little, and the tigar-snarl drew his lips hard against his teeth as he listened to the sounds filtering from the outer passage.

The heavy tread of metallic feet and the scream of a woman in an extremity of terror.

CHAPTER XVI

For a moment they stood shocked into silence then Lasser sprang to the door, his yellowed features contorted with emotion.

"No!" he gasped "No!"

"Lasser!" Wendis grabbed at the old man, his fingers slipping off the other's blouse, then the old doctor had jerked open the door and had run into the passage.

"Stop!" His thin voice almost broke with the intensity of his emotion. "Stop it I say. Rosslyn is…" His voice faded into silence and around him flared the vivid blue light of a para-beam.

"Lasser." Wendis gulped, then jerked back into the room as blue fire sprayed from down the corridor. "Curt! Help me!" Desperately he tugged at the narrow cot, flinging it in front of the open door and building a flimsy barricade of chairs and light furnishings. Curt helped him move a heavy desk. "The para-beam won't penetrate," gasped the young miner. "We can shelter behind this stuff and aim for their scanning eyes." He gulped as he saw the rigid body of the old doctor. "They're probably freezing every living thing in sight. They must want you an awful lot to do a thing like that."

"Let me give myself up." Curt shuddered as he remembered the pain of his own experience of the para-beam. "We can't let them kill all those people."

"They won't die," said Wendis grimly. "The revival squads will be standing by and this is no time to surrender." He drew back his lips in his tiger-snarl as he squinted through a crack in the barricade. "It's about time we had a show down anyway. Maybe we can send a few of them to hell before they get us." He grunted and the high velocity pistol in his hand fired with its spiteful explosion.

Numbly Curt crouched behind the flimsy shelter and waited for the metamen to advance.

He stared at them, reflected in the mirror finish of the polished door like figures from some incredible nightmare. Tall, with articulated limbs and a cone-shaped head. The para-beam seemed to emit from an orifice in their chests and the ruby light of their scanning eyes flared like the fires of hell. Unconsciously his finger tightened around the trigger of his weapon and a puff of incandescent vapour sprang from the wall where the tiny slug, moving at a tremendous velocity, expended its energy against the unyielding mass.

He grunted, and settled down to wait for a more vulnerable target.

It had begun with prosthetics, of course. First artificial arms, legs, then kidneys and hearing aids. Artificial lungs and mechanical aids to keep the heart beating. Electronic devices for use of the blind and cunningly fashioned wires to replace damaged nerves. Metal plates to shield a brain from harm, and metal splints to fasten broken bones.

He wondered when some genius had thought of uniting them all together.

It was logical, of course. Perhaps even too logical. All the old dreams of building a man-like robot had failed because no man had known how to build something compact enough to emulate the human brain. They had tried, and they had failed. Comain, the nearest approach to a mechanical brain, occupied ten square miles and used enough power to run a small city. Nothing either electronic or mechanical could even begin to rival a human brain for compactness and efficiency—and so…

They had built a mechanical body and used a human brain. Curt shuddered, wondering what they must feel like, those poor devils imprisoned in their unfeeling metal bodies. Perhaps they had volunteered, thinking that the loss of normal sensation and emotion would be compensated by their potential immortality and extended awareness. They could probably communicate between themselves by radio. They could see by means of the scanning eyes, hear via their diaphragms, even speak by transmitted electrical impulses, but they could never feel. They could never experience physical pleasure or pain. They would never know true emotion, for emotion is controlled by the glands and they had no glands. They were prisoners, trapped in their mobile hells, a few pounds of protoplasm served by machinery instead of by living flesh.

He wondered if they ever wished for death.

Something thrust itself against the barrier, the blue flame of the para-beam bringing a nerve-numbing chill, metal crumbling the flimsy shelter. Wendis snarled, a deep animal-like sound low in his throat, and the sound of his pistol mingled with his shouted instructions.

"The eyes. Curt! Aim for the eyes."

Fire stabbed from the tiny orifice of the high velocity pistol. A stream of slugs driving directly towards the ruby fire in the cone-shaped head. Incandescent vapour flared from the transparent plastic and the red glow died in a blue-white gush of electronic energy.

Abruptly the metaman halted, the blue fire of the para-beam dying with the ruby glow, and metal clashed as its articulated arms fell to its sides.

Like an obscene statue of man-like metal it stood in the doorway, and its silent body shimmered to the blue fire from its unharmed companions.

It wasn't dead. Somehow Curt knew that. The all-important brain hadn't been harmed but, as the cutting of a single wire immobilise a car, so the smashing of the scanning eyes had rendered the huge body impotent. Somewhere within that metal frame the brain still lived, in darkness and silence, waiting for a mechanic to restore light and awareness. Probably it was experiencing the nearest thing to death that it could ever know.

Again the pistol in his hand spat its lethal stream. Red fire yielded to electronic energy and over the clash of metal Curt could hear Wendis's fanatical curses. "How do you like the taste of that you damn robot? Come on, blast you! What are you waiting for?"

In the abrupt silence Curt could hear the sounds of the thudding metal, fading, dying into distance and silence. Startled he looked at the young miner.

"Have they gone?"

"I don't know." Wendis bit his lip and cautiously peered around the edge of the sagging barricade. "They can't be giving up, the metamen never do, and we've only stopped four of them." He glowered at the silent shapes of metal clogging the doorway. "You stay here, Curt. I'm going to have a look."

"Be careful," warned Curt anxiously. "They may have set a trap."

"Maybe." Wendis shrugged and moved towards the door. "There's only one way to find out." Carefully he slipped past a motionless figure and peered down the passage. "No signs of anything," he called softly. "I…" The sound of his pistol came simultaneously with a flaring swathe of blue.

"Wendis!" Curt sprang towards the door. "Are you alright?"

"Yes." Pain twisted the young miner's features as he nursed a limp arm. "The ray brushed me. I threw the thing off aim when I fired." He groaned, great beads of perspiration standing out against his skin, and Curt felt a quick sympathy with the young man as he began to massage the numb limb.

"Any chance of us getting out of here?"

"No." Wendis grunted as he flexed his fingers, wincing to the pain of returning circulation. "They've got a metaman placed at each end of the corridor. They'll keep us bottled up in here until they can fetch reinforcements, probably anaesthetic gas or a sonic beam."

"Then there's nothing we can do?"

"No." Wendis thinned his lips as he checked the loading of his pistol. "Personally I feel like making a rush for it. They're going to get us anyway and I'd feel a lot better if I could take some of them with me. We could rig up some shields from the furniture, and they would enable us to get close enough to shoot. With any luck at all we could break through the meta-men."

"And get away?" Curt shook his head. "No, Wendis. We might get a couple but what good would it do us? Why don't you let me give myself up?"

"Too late for that now. We've hidden you, they know it, and even if you were to walk out there now it would make no difference to how they treat us." Wendis glowered at the silent shapes of the halted metamen. "If they were only flesh and blood it would be different. What real harm can we do to those robots? But the Matriarch won't send humans, she values life too highly." He paused, his nostrils wrinkling as he sniffed at the air. "Smell anything?"

"No." Curt took a deep breath. "What makes you ask that?"

"Nothing. I…" Wendis snarled as something exploded with a soft thud outside the door. "Gas! Hold your breath, Curt. They're gassing us!"

From the open doorway a thin, milky white mist flowed into the room. It writhed, drifting through the still air as if it were a cloud of cigarette smoke, and as Curt sucked in a deep breath, he felt his senses reel.

Wendis ran towards the door, his pistol glinting in his hand. Narrow-eyed he stared through the swirling mist, then, his face red with the exertion of holding his breath, he staggered back across the room and towards the high windows. Savagely he jerked one open, gulping at the fresh air, and Curt, fighting desire to breathe at any cost, joined him.

"We've got to get out of here," gasped Wendis. He stared from the window and his eyes narrowed as he studied a ledge running along the front of the building. "How are your nerves Curt?" He pointed to the ledge. "If we can crawl along that ledge to the corner, then climb up the ornamentation towards the roof, we might stand a chance of getting away. Luckily we're on the top floor, and they won't be able to use gas once we're in the open."

Curt shuddered, looking down at the street far below. He hesitated, and as he did so, the mist seeped around them and from the corridor came the heavy sound of metallic feet.

"Let's go."

Lithely Wendis crawled out of the window and dropped on to the ledge. He swayed a moment, then, his face wet with perspiration, regained his balance and began to inch along the narrow strip of concrete. Curt followed him, the HV pistol pressing against his stomach from where he had thrust it into his belt, and around them, pushing like tiny hands, a faint wind blew from the West.

It wasn't really hard, thought Curt grimly. It was no more difficult than walking along a nine inch plank laid on the ground. But somehow he couldn't forget the thousand feet drop waiting just behind him, the tiny figures of staring people in the street below, the mess he would make if he slipped or staggered away from the wall. He could see it before him, two inches from his eyes, and he pressed his hands against it as he sidled along, poising on the balls of his feet, rubbing the stone with his chest and thighs, refusing with a grim determination to yield to the temptation of looking downwards.

Suddenly he bumped into Wendis.

The young man had stopped, half around the corner of the building, and Curt could see the sweat glistening on his features.

"Now for the hard part." The young man grinned, a savage baring of his teeth, and the rising winds seemed to catch his words and whip them away. "I'll go first. If we can manage to climb to that overhang, get over it, then reach that cornice and pull ourselves on to the roof we'll be safe. Think you can do it?"

"I can try." Curt licked his lips and kept his eyes fastened on the smooth stone before him. "Hurry, will you. I can't take too much of this."

Wendis grunted and reached for an ornamented piece of stone.

Impatiently Curt waited for Wendis to climb up and out of the way. He stood, his head turned back along the way they had come, his cheek pressed against the smooth stone. He was trembling, his muscles jumping with re-action and fear, and within his chest his heart thudded with an almost pain-ful violence. Surely the metamen would have reached the room by now? They would have crossed it, unaffected by the anaesthetic gas. They would have seen the open window, known what it meant, they...

He almost screamed as a cone-shaped head thrust itself from the open window and ruby fight flared as the metaman scanned the narrow ledge.

Tensely he waited. Afraid to move. Afraid to twist his body, drag the pistol from his belt and fire at the red glow of the scanning eyes. He waited, almost sick with dread, for the blue fire of the para-beam to stiffen his body and send him plunging to his death a thousand feet below.

It didn't come.

The flaring red glow of the scanning eyes steadied as the metaman stared at him. For an awful moment Curt hovered on the brink of destruc-tion as his fear-tensed muscles caused him to sway away from the safety of the building, then understanding came, and with it a flood of relief. They wanted him alive. The blue ray didn't kill, not immediately, and the gas was relatively harmless. The only danger he was in was of his own making and he felt sweat trickle down his back as he relaxed and tried to ignore the cold glare of the robot-like things staring at him.

From above came the spiteful sound of a high velocity pistol on auto-matic fire.

Incandescent vapour exploded from the cone-shaped head. Plastic yielded to the impact of slugs moving at tremendous velocity, and a gush of electronic blue flame replaced the red glow of the scanning eyes. Abruptly the metaman slumped and from the room came the faint sounds of clanging metal.

"Curt!" Wendis's voice was thin and distant as he called against the rising wind. "Hurry. Before another one comes."

Obediently Curt reached upwards and began to climb the corner of the building.

It was a nightmare. It was a thing he had dreamed about before he discovered his innate fear of heights. Sweat moistened his palms, trickled down his face, stung his eyes and turned his fingers into slippery claws. His feet fumbled as he forced them against the stone, and the droning wind seemed to get between him and the building, forcing him outwards to gulf below.

Above him he heard Wendis's snarling curse.

Fear replaced the savage anger. "Curt! I can't make it! I can't get over the overhang!"

"What's wrong?" Curt gritted his teeth as he forced himself to stare upwards.

"My arms aren't long enough to get a grip. Curt I'm falling!"

"Hold on!" Grimly the young man climbed upwards. "I'll get below you, take a good grip, and you can rest your foot on my head. Get as high as you can."

"Right. But hurry, Curt. Hurry."

Curt winced to the desperation in the other's voice. If Wendis lost his grip, slipped, fell from where he clung to the ornamented stone, he would strike Curt and together they would plunge to the street a thousand feet below. Frantically he glanced to either side of where he clung. Aside from the ornamentation at the corner the building was a smooth surface of sheer stone, broken only by the narrow ledge far below. His only chance was to retreat, climb down to the ledge and crawl away from the corner, but he knew that he couldn't do that, knew that long before he reached the ledge his fingers would slip or Wendis would fall.

He grunted as a boot struck him on the side of the head.

"Ready?" He reached for a handhold and pressed himself tight against the stone. "Now. Rest your foot on my head. I'm going to surge upwards and I want you to make a grab at the next hold. We'll move together when I shout. Understand?"

"What if I miss, Curt? We'll both go down."

"If you fall we'll both go anyway. Now! Ready?"

"Yes."

"Now!"

Desperately he surged upwards, trying to ignore the crushing pressure against his skull, clawing at the ornamentation with a grim frenzy, and fighting the down and outwards thrust of the other's foot. For a moment it seemed that they had failed. For a moment the wind droned between Curt and the building, and he could hear the sounds of the other's rasping breath. Then the pressure had gone, the wind no longer whined before him, and, his heart pounding against his ribs and the cold sweat of fear trickling down his face, he pressed himself against the stone.

"Made it." Wendis made the words sound like a prayer. "You all right, Curt?"

"Yes." He bit his lips as tormented muscles relayed their messages of pain. "What now?"

"I'll climb up to the roof. Strip-off my clothes and make a rope, then lower it down to you. Can you hold on for a few more minutes?"

"I don't know." Curt tasted the warm saltiness of blood from his bitten lips. "Hurry!"

He waited. He waited while aching muscles weakened and within his skull his brain seemed limned in fire. A peculiar numbness came over him, as if all he did and felt was somehow unreal. It would be such a little thing. Just a brief gust of wind, a painless fall, then a sudden shock and an eternity of rest. It would be better than this mind-twisting fear, this torment of outraged flesh and quivering muscles. It would be death, but what was that? A dark encounter, and to him, it would be as if he met an old friend. He grinned a little, his lips twisting without humour, as he pondered what seemed be an important question.

Can the dead die? He had died once. He had gone into the great dark and the deep unknown, and death and he were strangers. He had died, and been resurrected, and of all men he should be the least to fear the ultimate ending. He...

Something whipped across his face. A long, thin, slender rope of twisted cloth. Knotted, crude, a thing of hasty construction and desperate hope. It swayed before him, stirred by the droning wind, and he stared at it for a full second before he realised what it was. Then he grabbed it, and signalled with a long tug.

"Ready?" Wendis's voice mingled with the droning wind, tattered and weak. "Hang on, Curt. I'll have you safe in half a minute."

Grimly Curt clutched hold of the crude rope as the young man heaved on the other end. Slowly the building fell before him, the ornamentation, the overhang, the cornice. Curt sagged with relief as he saw the rim of the roof, grinned as he watched the almost naked figure of the young man drawing in the rope, then felt burning tension and sick fear as he saw something else.

A tall thing, metallic, ruby light flaring from its cone-shaped head, and articulated arms outstretched towards the sweat-marked figure of the young miner.

Desperately he grabbed at his waist, fumbling for the smooth butt of the high velocity pistol. He clamped his teeth on his instinctive shout of warning and fear clawed at him as the metaman came closer to Wendis. If he shouted. If Wendis turned and saw what was behind him. If the thing used the para-beam now, when he was still hanging helpless at the end of a rope, hanging suspended over a thousand foot drop… Curt swallowed and clawed at the gun.

He touched it, felt the smooth metal of the butt, then his sweat-covered fingers slipped off the smooth metal and he knew the sickness of despair as the gun went spinning to the street below.

Wendis turned and saw the metaman.

He turned, and the rope sagged from his startled grasp. He turned—and the blue fire of the para-beam stiffened him into wooden rigidity.

Then Curt was falling a thousand feet to the street below.

He dropped past the cornice. He fell past the overhang and the wind droned louder in his ears as he stared numbly at the tiny, ant-like figures of people far below. Then something almost tore the rope from his lax fingers, spinning him like a weight at the end of a line, jerking at his arms and sending waves of pain from his shoulder sockets.

Swiftly he rose again towards the safety of the roof. He rose with almost incredible speed and before his shocked senses could register what must have happened he felt the firmness of the roof beneath him, and, almost collapsing from reaction and strain, sagged forward.

Something gripped him firmly around the waist, preventing his fall, and steadying him against something hard and firm.

Dully he stared at the glint of metal, the smooth, articulated metal of a metaman's arms.

CHAPTER XVII

Sarah Bowman sat at her desk and stared at a calendar with sombre eyes. In the early morning light she seemed haggard, with dark circles beneath her eyes and lines of worry and indecision scored deep into the surface of her mannish features. A videophone screen flared into colourful life and the old Matriarch stared dully at the picture of her receptionist.

"Madam?"

"What do you want?"

"Your secretary is here, Madam. Shall I admit her?"

"Yes."

"Very good, Madam." The screen dulled, swirled with fading colour; then resumed its normal gleaming blankness. Softly the door opened and Nyeeda entered the office.

She wore her usual black and her hair and skin displayed their normal, well-tended-for grooming, but, like the old woman sitting at the desk, she seemed tired and overstrained. Slowly she crossed the room, sitting in a vacant chair, and as she sat the light from the high windows glittered from the wide band of intricately fashioned gold she wore at her wrist.

"Well?" The Matriarch spoke without looking at the young girl. "Is everything under control?"

"Yes, Madam." Nyeeda sighed and gently massaged her temples with the tips of her slender fingers. "All the Martians have been captured and re-registered with Comain. The unknown force has been found. Every person in the city and every person who could possibly have been in contact with the Martians has been traced and has donned the helmet. Aside from the extra man Comain has full data about everyone, and, as soon as the registration is complete, things will be as the used to be."

"Normal you mean?"

"Yes, Madam."

"Good." The old woman sighed, and, as if moving of their own volition, her eyes turned to the calendar. "Have you discovered anything about this 'extra man'?"

"His name is Rosslyn, Curt Rosslyn. He was discovered by two Asteroid Miners adrift in space and revived at the Martian settlement. Their nominal head, a Doctor Lasser, had the idea of keeping his presence a secret. Though he doesn't admit it I believe that he hoped the extra man would so upset the predictions of Comain that we would agree to sending the colonists back to Mars in order to end the nuisance."

"He made a nuisance of himself all right," said the Matriarch grimly. "Anything else?"

"Yes. This man Rosslyn is a 'freak'. By that, of course, I mean a freak survival. He actually lived in the days before the Atom War, before Comain even. He was the pilot on an experimental Moon flight. His ship was wrecked, the hull split, and he died instantly from loss of heat and asphyxiation. It was a miracle that he was ever found, another that he was revived. No wonder he could upset the predictions so much. Why the man knows nothing of our civilisation at all."

"The Martians of course thought to use him as a tool." The Matriarch nodded. "So much for the mystery of the 'unknown force'. Has he been registered?"

"Not yet."

"Why not?"

"Since his capture three days ago he has been in state of coma." Nyeeda flushed a little beneath the critical gaze of the old woman. "I admit that I could have revived him, but I thought it best to leave him alone. If you have read my reports you will know that he and one of the Martians, a man named Wendis, fought and immobilised four of the metamen. They tried to escape by climbing from their room to the roof of the building. Rosslyn almost died, if the metaman hadn't grabbed his rope and broken his fall he would have been smashed to pieces. The experience gave him a tremendous mental trauma. Add that to his undoubted confusion at being thrust into an unfamiliar environment, his physical weakness and the, as yet unknown, effects of exposure to the free radiations of outer space for more than two centuries, and you will understand why I decided to leave him alone. More shocks may irreparably damage his mind and it won't hurt for us to wait a few more hours before registering him with Comain."

"You think so?" Again the Matriarch stared at the calendar. "For you perhaps a few hours may make no difference, but not for others. Why wasn't he registered?"

"I told you!" Nyeeda winced at the raw emotion and naked hate in the old woman's tone. "He was in a state of coma. What should I have done, killed him?"

"Better that than leave him as a permanent threat to our safety."

"He can do no harm now. An unconscious man cannot be registered and when he awakes I will lead him straight to the machine. You have nothing to fear, Madam."

"No?" Again the old woman stared at the calendar and something, a peculiar blending of fear and a horrible kind of fascination, glowed for a moment in her faded eyes. "Sometimes, Nyeeda, I think that you are a fool. At other times I am certain of it. You say that it can make no difference, that a few hours can't hurt anyone; that a day or so doesn't matter. Fool! Look at the date, girl. Look at it."

"Well?" Nyeeda stared blankly at the calendar. "What of it?"

"It means nothing to you does it? Just another day, one of several thousand which you still hope to enjoy. Just a mark on a calendar. Well, maybe it means nothing to you, but to me..." The old woman paused and again the mingling of opposed emotions glowed in her faded eyes. "To me," she whispered. "It means death."

"Death?"

"Yes, fool! Death!"

"But...?"

"Comain can predict many things," said the old woman, and it was as if she spoke to herself more than to the girl sitting at her desk. "It can predict the success of a harvest, the probability of a storm, the result of an experiment. It can predict the life of a building, the endurance of a machine, the extent to which any fabrication can be relied on. Comain can predict all these things. Comain can foretell what must be and it can do it to within 99.9999999 percent of probability. It can do all these things I say—if it has all the data."

"I know that," said Nyeeda, uncomfortably. "Everyone knows that."

"So," continued the old woman, and it was as if Nyeeda had never spoken. "If a machine can do all that isn't it reasonable to expect it to do a little more? If, with all the available data, it can predict to a day, to an hour even, the durability of a piece of steel, couldn't it do more? Couldn't it perhaps predict the life span of a man or of a woman? Couldn't it state that at a certain time a certain person would reach the end of her days?" She stared at Nyeeda and the girl shuddered to what she saw glowing in the old woman's eyes. "Answer me, girl! Could it do all that?"

"I don't know, Madam. I..."

"Yes, girl. You do know. How many times have you been tempted to ask about your own future? How many times have you hesitated before asking the one question the answer to which would have made your life a living misery? How often have you wondered just when you would die?"

It was true. Nyeeda knew it, knew too that the old woman had read her innermost thoughts. The temptation was always there, only the fact that all her questions to Comain were recorded, that, and a secret fear of doubting her own inner strength had prevented her from asking the fatal question. Silently she stared at the old woman and a great pity for the Matriarch stung her eyes with unshed tears.

"For the Matriarch it is easy," whispered the old woman. "She can ask any question she wishes. She has access to Comain here, in her own office, and there is no need to descend to the lower levels of fear that her questions will be recorded. Perhaps years pass before she ever thinks about it. Ten years, twenty, even more, but, day after day, hour after hour, the temptation is there, waiting. Years pass and she grows old. More years pass and still there is so much to do, so many things to direct, to change, to alter. So many things. Too many. And so the temptation grows and grows and grows. It would be so simple to ask. To end the gnawing doubt, to get some idea so that the essential work could be completed in a single lifetime. It would be so easy, just one simple question and all doubt, all fear, all hesitation would be over for ever."

Something like a sob echoed through the room and Nyeeda winced to the pain in the old woman's eyes.

"I asked the question. It must have been twenty years ago now. Twenty years. To me at that time it seemed as if I had an eternity of life before me. Then, as the years passed, as age and senility added their weight to gnawing fear, desperation came. Daily I questioned Comain. Daily I had my answer and, as the time lessened, so the probability increased, nines! Three. Five. Seven. Nine. Certainty!"

The old voice broke as it rose and the last word came out as a ragged scream. Silence followed, a deep silence broken only by the rasping echo of a woman sobbing with dry eyes and a breaking heart.

"Can you imagine what I suffered? Can you even begin to know the desperation, the frenzy, the futile longing and forlorn hope? I tried altering what I had planned deliberately doing my best to make the predictions inaccurate, changing data as much as possible to vary the original predictions my life span. It was for that reason I recalled the Martian colonists. I had hoped that with more than five hundred new sets of data, five hundred new influences in the world, some in some un-guessable way, the original time limit would be extended. I was wrong."

"You mean that there has been no change?" For the time the Matriarch seemed to remember that she was not alone and she stared at Nyeeda with haggard eyes.

"No. No change. No change even though all the colonists have been re-registered and all the city, too. No change though we have had fighting and open rebellion. No change even though we have among us a man risen from the dead."

"But he hasn't been registered yet." Nyeeda felt a surge of excitement as she stared at the Matriarch. "Rosslyn is still an unknown factor."

"What!" Hope flared in the faded eyes. "Yes. Yes, of course, I had forgotten. Bring him here, Nyeeda. Stab his brain with electricity if you have to, drug him, do anything as long as he is conscious and can be registered. Bring him to me. Hurry."

"Yes, Madam." The girl hesitated. "Have I a time limit?"

"Get him here as soon as possible." Anger flared in the haggard eyes. "I…" The Matriarch winced, almost falling from her chair, and clutching at the region of her heart. She sagged, her skin turning a peculiar shade of grey, and her breath whistled between her clenched teeth. Startled, Nyeeda sprang to her feet and stooped over the old woman.

"Madam! You are ill. Let me call a doctor."

"No!" Grimly the Matriarch struggled upright on her chair. "Leave me. It is nothing, a pain I get at times, almost as if a hand is clutching at my heart. Leave me now. I still have time." Her pain-filled eyes stared at the clock hanging against one wall. It was a beautiful piece of mechanism, electronically operated and warning of the passing hours by means of a deep chime.

"I still have an hour," whispered the old woman desperately. "Comain can't fail me now, not after twenty years. I shall die in one hour's time, at eleven o'clock, Comain predicted it." She gasped, and perspiration shone thickly against her greyish skin. "Hurry, girl. Get Rosslyn here. Get him here conscious and aware." Urgently she pushed Nyeeda towards the door.

"Get Rosslyn!"

She slumped again as the secretary left the room, and her eyes, as she stared at the wide face of the clock, held all terror and all fear.

She had one hope left.

CHAPTER XVIII

Deep within the building which was Comain, in a windowless cell with a barred door and a single light, Curt Rosslyn sat and let his mind writhe like a thing alive within the confines of his skull. Of the passage of time he knew nothing. Of where he was and why he was here the same. Between his capture by the metaman and his awakening in this cell lay a blank period, a flame-shot time of dulled senses, of inner pain and a numb, half-aware realisation of peculiar changes and agonising rebirth.

Now he sat and struggled to bring order out of chaos.

It was his mind, he knew that, knew too that in some indefinable way the blasting radiations of outer space had changed him while he rested in frozen death within the confines of his wrecked ship. He had been half-aware of it before, his ability to direct the fall of dice and the spin of a ball, his fumbling efforts to move the tiny leaf while sitting in the park, those thing warned him that he was not as other men, not as he used to be.

Now...

Pain traced fiery paths through his aching skull, and the back of his head seemed to be splitting from internal pressure. It was as if the normally unused portions of the brain, the nine tenths which seemed to serve no useful function, had acquired feeling and awareness, and Curt pressed the heels of his palms to his throbbing skull as he stared down at the smooth concrete floor of his cell.

Telekinesis. The ability to direct the movements of inanimate objects by mental power alone. He had that ability. Somehow he had acquired it during his centuries-long journey exposed to the free radiations of outer space, and, if he had acquired one such power, what other unsuspected abilities rested within his activated brain? Teleportation perhaps? The ability to move himself through space with no other aid than his mental a of paraphysical science. Telepathy? He frowned as he thought about it, he wasn't sure that he would like to be able to read the minds of other people.

Irritably he relaxed and stared at the single bulb illuminating the cell. Electrons, he thought, tiny particles speeding at almost the velocity of fight along a wire. Perhaps...

The fight went out.

In the darkness he grinned and felt unsuspected neuron paths open in the normally unused portions of his brain. It was simple. If it were possible to control dice and ball and leaf, how much simpler must it be to control a tiny thing like an electron? He directed his thoughts and abruptly the fight flared with eye-searing brilliance, then, as he adjusted the flow, softened into its normal glow.

So much for that.

The door came next. Suddenly the barred portal sagged against the jamb, the heavy metal bars bowing as to the impact of a tremendous force, and the steady glow of the single bulb flared and wavered in a confused alternation of light and darkness. Curt groaned and slumped on to the narrow bed, blood seeping from his bitten lips and his hands pressed tight against the throbbing agony of his skull.

For a moment he thought that he was going to die, and, so great was his pain, he would have welcomed death for the mercy of its oblivion. A sound forced its way past his clenched teeth, a raw, animal-like sound, a cry born of the ultimate torment the mind and body of man can endure, and his muscles jerked and quivered in uncontrolled reflexes beneath his sweat-soaked skin.

Slowly the pain died, and, almost sick with weakness and reaction, Curt rested on the narrow cot and stared curiously at the barred door. Why had he felt such torment? How was it that he could control the flow of electrons and yet, when he had tried to wrench open the door, he had suffered such agony? Understanding came and his lips writhed with self-contempt at his own stupidity.

He had been a fool!

He was like a child with the muscles of a man, or, more correctly, a moron playing with new powers. An electron was a tiny thing, its mass almost undetectable, and it needed little to alter its flow. But it still had mass and he had forgotten that. His mental force was new, untried, untrained. He had tasted success and had rushed in to test his powers without thought or any exercise of logic. Like a child who found he could lift a, to him, heavy weight he had tried to move the mass of many tons. The door was of metal, a hard adamantine metal, with thick bars and interlaced strips. He had tried to move it with brute force and his mental energy had recoiled upon itself. Like a man who attempts to drive his muscles too far, he had suffered a form of mental, muscle-strain, and he had paid for it.

He gritted his teeth and again the light dimmed, flared, died and resumed its normal glow. Again he concentrated on the door, but this time with caution, letting his mind probe and feel. Deep down inside his brain something seemed to scratch the surface of his awareness, like a tiny finger irritating the delicate structure of his brain, like the nagging presence of a half-forgotten thought. He frowned, trying to ignore it, concentrating on the mass of metal barring his way to freedom. Again it bowed, thrusting from the jamb and straining at its multiple locks. Again pain seared him, burning along the neuron paths and bringing sweat to his chilly flesh with the promise of hell to come. Hastily he retracted his thoughts, frowning as the nagging irritation probed within his skull, and he concentrated on it, turning his thoughts inward, and yet, at the same time, keeping his resolve to open the door to the forefront of his consciousness.

The irritation grew, seemed to sparkle with tiny bursts of mental energy, and—the door swung open.

For a moment Curt stared at it, noting the shining surfaces of the severed locking bars and the easily poised weight of the metal lattice. He smiled as understanding came, and, like a child playing with a new toy, caused the door to swing on its well-oiled hinges.

After a while he rose and walked into the deserted corridor of his cell.

A second barred door opened to his new-found trick of mental concentration and he walked casually towards a short flight of stairs. Something stirred in an alcove, a metallic thing with articulated arms and a cone-shaped head. It stirred, ruby light flaring from its scanning eyes, then metal clashed as it collapsed on to the concrete floor, its articulated limbs sprawled and useless. Curt ignored it, his mind already probing the intricacies of the locked door of an elevator. He tensed as his ears caught the hum of machinery, and his mind sharpened to the approach of sentient beings. For a moment he hesitated, not yet fully confident in his own powers to risk teleportation, and, as he stood in doubt before the elevator, the door swung open and he stared at the startled features of a dark-haired woman.

"Rosslyn!" Nyeeda leapt from the cage and behind her, female guards lifted their weapons in automatic reflex action, the tiny orifices of the high velocity pistols centred on his stomach. "Rosslyn! How did you get here?"

He shrugged, his eyes narrowed as he stared at the menacing weapons. He could disarm the guards, he knew that. He a wrench the pistols from their hands, dash them against the unyielding metal of the wall, step over their broken bodies to the elevator and to—what? Not freedom. Not the calm acceptance of these people as an equal. Not to the safety of friends and the comfort of a place in this civilisation. He could escape, but what point was there in continually running from a danger he only suspected? If they had wanted him dead they could have killed him long ago, but, despite all that he had been told, they had saved his life and there seemed no immediate reason to doubt their intentions. He stared at the woman.

"Who are you?"

"Nyeeda. Secretary to the Matriarch. But how did you get here?" She frowned as she saw the sprawled figure of the metaman. "Fenshaw! Call the guards."

"Yes, Madam." One of the women sheathed her weapon and pressing a stud on her belt whispered into a tiny disc strapped to her wrist. "Shall we return the prisoner to his cell?"

"No." Nyeeda bit her lips as she stared at the calm features of the man. "You stay here. You others escort us to the Matriarch. Rosslyn. You will come with me. At once!"

"Will I?" Deliberately he folded his arms, smiling into the perfect features of the dark-haired woman. "Why should I?"

"Because if you don't I'll have the guards rip your body open with HV slugs." Something ugly glowed for a moment in the midnight of her eyes and Curt grinned as he recognised her emotion for what it was.

"I don't think that you will do that," he said calmly. "You're worried aren't you? Why?"

"Please." Nyeeda glanced impatiently towards the elevator. "Come with me now without question or argument. You will not be harmed, that I promise, but please waste no more time."

"To the Matriarch?"

"Yes."

"I see." Curt shrugged and stepped towards the elevator. "You know of me I take it? You know how I arrived here?"

"We know all about you." Nyeeda gestured towards the guards, and, as they crowded into the cage, slammed the door and stabbed at the control buttons with her slender fingers.

"I'm glad of that," said Curt quietly. "Am I being taken for trial?"

"No."

"To freedom then?"

"Please!" Nyeeda stared at him with desperate intensity. "We have no time for argument. You will not be harmed, but you must do as directed, and do it at once. If not…" She fell silent but her eyes were expressive as she glanced towards the watching guards.

"You would kill me?" Curt smiled and the woman flushed as she read the emotion in his grey eyes. "I think not—Nyeeda? Is that your name?"

"It is."

"A nice name," mused Curt. He stared unabashedly at her dark beauty. "I think that we shall be seeing much of each other, Nyeeda."

"I doubt it," she snapped curtly. "I am Secretary to the Matriarch."

"And I," he said quietly, "am the friend of Comain."

He smiled into her questioning eyes.

CHAPTER XIX

The elevator opened directly into the office of the Matriarch and Curt stared curiously about him as the dark-haired woman dismissed the guards and slammed the door of the cage. He stood, a rumpled figure in his torn slacks and blouse, and his slender body seemed vibrant with a new strength as he stared at the ruler of Earth with his peculiar scintillant grey eyes. In turn Sarah Bowman stared at the man who was her one hope of life.

She had aged in the past thirty minutes, her cheeks sagging and her faded eyes burning with desperation. Against one wall the wide face of the electronic clock seemed to stare at her with inner mockery, and, feeling stifled in the confines of the room, she had flung open the high windows. They led on to a small terrace, a piece of architecture designed for ornamental rather than utilitarian purposes, but the builders had raised a low rampart along its edge and sometimes, in the cool of evening or the soft warmth of night, the Matriarch used it as a vantage point from which to survey the city and surrounding plain.

"Does he know?" She snapped the question, her eyes never leaving the calm features of the man. Nyeeda shook her head.

"No, Madam. Shall I inform him?"

"No you fool!" Savagely the old woman pulled herself upright and rose from her chair. "That would take time, too much time, and I have so little now. So little."

"As you wish, Madam." Nyeeda stepped forward to assist the old woman.

"Get away from me, girl! Watch the man. I can manage."

Slowly the old woman moved from behind her wide desk and halted before a panel set flush into the wall. She pressed her palm against it, spreading her fingers against the sensitised plate, and, as the electronic scanning eye recognised the lines of her palm, the door slid silently aside revealing a small cubicle.

Within that cubicle was Comain.

Curt stared at the ruby lit scanning eye, the dull metal helmet, the low bench and easy chair. It seemed to be a copy of the one he had tried to use in the city but there were subtle differences though the basics remained the same.

"Will you register the man first, Madam?"

"No. I'll consult Comain first. Then Rosslyn can don the helmet and I'll consult the machine again. If he can alter the original prediction I will give him anything he may desire. Anything and everything this entire planet can supply. He can ask for the world and it will be his, but, if the original prediction remains..." Something flared in the faded old eyes. "He shall die."

"Am I to have no say in the matter?" Curt stared at the old woman.

"No."

He shrugged and watched interestedly as she sat in the easy chair and threw a contact.

"Yes?" The metallic, inhuman voice echoed clearly through the room.

"Information. Unrestricted level. It is the Matriarch who speaks." The old woman rested her bared left wrist against the scanning eye.

"Yes?"

"Predict my death."

For a moment there was silence and in the strained hush Curt could hear the sharp inhalation of the dark-haired woman at his side.

"Prediction as to death of Matriarch. Death within thirty minutes."

"Be more explicit. Predict hour of death."

"Prediction of death of Matriarch. Hour of death. Eleven o'clock General Standard Time. Probability nine nines."

The mechanical voice stopped and for a moment the woman sagged over the low bench, her shoulders bowed and her hands trembling as they gripped the arms of her chair, moving with an almost painful effort, she rose and stared at Curt.

"Register the man."

"Yes, Madam." Nyeeda stepped towards the cubicle. "This way. Hurry."

"No."

"What?" She stared at the Matriarch. "Please don't be foolish. You must register with Comain. Now hurry!"

"I refuse." Curt smiled at the consternation in her eyes and deliberately sat on the edge of the wide desk. "Certain threats have been uttered," he said calmly. "To be frank with you I don't know yet what this is all about, but it seems that you want me to do something. Am I right?"

"Yes."

"Well then, if I do it, what's in it for me?"

"You will register with Comain." The Matriarch stepped towards the young man and naked hate distorted her sagging features. "I will not bargain with you, but know this. Unless you agree to register you will be shot. Nyeeda! Call the guards."

"Wait." Curt slipped from the edge of the desk. "Will my dead body help you?"

"It will not harm me if that's what you hope." The Matriarch panted as she stared at the wide face of the electronic clock. "Fifteen minutes left. Register. Register before I kill you with my own hands!" Curt blinked, staring at a small pistol which had appeared in the old woman's hands. He stared at it, then raising his eyes, looked directly into distorted face of the Matriarch. "You leave me little choice," he said calmly. "What is it you want me to do?"

"Show him, Nyeeda."

"Yes, Madam." The Secretary pointed towards the cubicle. "Sit in that chair. Place the helmet over your head. I will attend to the rest."

Silently Curt sat in the easy chair and lifted the helmet.

It was of some dull metal, lined with what seemed to be sponge platinum. A cable led from it, a thick, insulated cable, and it covered his entire skull like the appliances used for drying hair in his own period. He donned it and Nyeeda stooped over his shoulder as she threw several switches.

"Fresh registration. Probe deep and record all data."

A red lamp blinked on a wall panel and the girl sighed as she turned to the Matriarch "Registration completed, Madam."

"Good." The old woman glared at Curt. "Well? What are you waiting for? Get out of that chair."

Silently he obeyed, a puzzled frown creasing his forehead and a speculative expression in his grey eyes. He had felt nothing, no probe of current, no tangible sensation of surging energy, nothing to denote that the contents of his mind had been copied and transferred to the memory banks of Comain.

Tensely the Matriarch sat in the chair and identified herself to the machine.

"Yes?"

"Predict death of the Matriarch."

"Prediction of death. Life span will terminate at eleven o'clock. Probability nine nines."

"What!" Desperately the old woman cleared the panel and re-identified herself. "Predict my death on the basis of all available data. All available data."

Silence for a moment as if the machine were searching through a million stored memories and ten million filed references. In the silence Curt could hear the ragged breathing of the old woman, and beside him, her lips parted with anticipation, the secretary leaned a little forward.

"Prediction as to death." The cold, unhuman voice from the speaker echoed through the room. "Death at eleven o'clock. Probability nine nines."

"So!" All life seemed to drain from the old woman as she slumped over the low bench. "Nine nines probability that I will die at eleven o'clock." A choked sound came from her throat, then, as if finally accepting the inevitable, she straightened and left the cubicle. "You realise what this means, Nyeeda?"

"A nine nines probability has always been certainty." The secretary licked her bps with a nervous gesture and glanced at the wide face of the electronic clock. The Matriarch followed her gaze.

"Five minutes," she said calmly. "In all my experience the machine has never been wrong with full data to work on." She stared at Curt and the pistol glinted with silent menace in her hand. "I should kill you. I should blast you down like a mad dog as I promised, but…" She shrugged and the tiny orifice of the muzzle twisted and slewed upwards and inwards.

"No!" Nyeeda lunged forward. "No, Madam. You can't!"

"Why not? Comain has predicted my death. You know what that means. Why wait for the end? Why hang on to the last few minutes? Why not end it all—now."

"No!" Curt didn't move but the pistol seemed to jerk, to twist, to fall and thud softly on to the carpeted floor. "Are you insane, old woman? Kill yourself and you make the prediction come true. Is that what you want? Are you so afraid of Comain being wrong that you will die rather than admit he could be at fault?"

"Comain is never wrong."

"Then you will die." He was deliberately cruel. "Why hasten the inevitable? You have two minutes yet. Believe me, Madam, death can last an awfully long time. Why not enjoy those last two minutes while you can?"

She hesitated, staring at the pistol which had so strangely left her hand, then, as she noticed the high windows and the sunlit terrace outside, she nodded.

"You are right," she whispered. "It is such a little time, but…" Slowly she stepped to the windows, breathing deeply of the warm air as she passed through them onto the terrace, then, standing close to the low rampart, she stared out over the city of Comain.

Against the wall the hands of the electronic clock moved towards the fatal hour.

"She will die," whispered Nyeeda, and Curt felt her slender body quiver as, instinctively, she pressed against him.

"Perhaps." He stared at the clock then focused his eyes and mind on the figure of the old Matriarch as she stood by the low rampart of the sunlit terrace.

"She will die," repeated Nyeeda sickly. "Now." Together with her words came the soft chiming of the electronic clock.

One. Two. Three.

On the terrace the old woman swayed a little as she heard the chiming of the fatal hour.

Six. Seven. Eight.

The swaying increased. She gasped, clutching at her chest, her sagging features grey with pain and fear, then, slowly at first but with accelerating speed, she crumpled, swayed, hit the low edge of the rampart—and toppled forward into space.

Nyeeda screamed, a chill, soul-wrenching sound, jarring from the walls and the furnishings of the office, echoing and skirling in shocked realisation.

Curt grunted and concentrated on the itching at the back of his brain.

Incredibly the old woman did not fall. She hovered, her body limp and helpless, suspended five thousand feet above the plain below, and sweat started in great beads on Curt's forehead as he fought his instinctive desire to run forward and grasp the Matriarch. Slowly, as if blown by a gentle wind, the limp figure of the old woman moved back on to the terrace, away from the low rampart and the certain death waiting below. She drifted, bobbed a little, then, with a startling gentleness, came to rest on the smooth surface of the terrace.

Ten. Eleven.

In the silence following the ending of the chimes Nyeeda's breathing sounded harsh and loud as if she had just run a dozen miles. She staggered, almost fell, then, with an almost savage explosion of energy, she had run from the room and was stooping over the figure of the old woman.

Tensely Curt waited while the slender fingers rested on the heart, touched the wrist, then lingered, almost caressingly, on the great vein in the wrinkled throat.

"She's alive." Incredulous amazement made the secretary's voice shrill and almost ugly. "She's alive!"

"Yes," said Curt. He wiped his streaming forehead and slumped down on to the edge of the wide desk.

"But she can't be alive. She can't be." Nyeeda stared at the young man. "Comain said that she would die. The machine predicted it. She can't be alive. She can't be!"

"She is." Curt pointed towards the feebly twitching figure of the Matriarch. "She is alive and will stay that way only has the sense to see a doctor about her heart."

"But…" The secretary rose and her eyes as she stared at Curt held a peculiar horror. "Only one thing could have saved her," she whispered. "An unknown factor. You donned the helmet, and yet, even though you had registered, you saved Matriarch from certain death. Comain should have known of your power. The data should have been recorded, but…" Her voice died in silence as she realised just what she was saying.

"You didn't register! In some way Comain didn't transfer the contents of your brain. You are still a danger to our safety, still an unknown force." She stepped forward and Curt winced to the emotion mirrored on her perfect features. "You are still an extra man."

Abruptly she turned and ran towards the door.

"Wait." Curt smiled as she spun and moved towards him. "Do not call your guards. I would hate to kill them, but, if you call them and they threaten me I will not be gentle."

"You…" Again she twisted and ran towards the door. Curt sighed, concentrated on the itching at the back of his brain, and smiled into her startled eyes.

"Relax," he said gently. "There is nothing to get upset about. Hadn't you better look after the old woman?"

"Who are you?" whispered the girl. "What are you?"

"I told you once," he said evenly. "I told you in the elevator along with something else. Can you remember what it was?"

"No."

"You're lying. I said that you and I would be seeing much of each other. I am not boasting, neither am I telling you anything but what you yourself have thought. If you are honest you will admit that. Well?"

"You devil!" Anger flushed her pale features. "Can you read minds as well?"

"As well as what?"

"You know what I mean." She flushed again and stared thoughtfully at the young man. "I remember now. You said that you were a friend of Comain. What did you mean by that?"

"I said that I am the friend of Comain," said Curt evenly. "And I meant exactly what I said." He slipped from his perch on the edge of the desk and glanced at the Matriarch, now sitting up and staring wildly about her. "Fetch her in, soothe her; calm her down. We have important matters to discuss."

"Such as?"

"Such as the future of this world." He smiled a little at her expression, then, moving with a casual assurance, he stepped behind the wide desk and sat down.

In the chair of the Matriarch.

CHAPTER XX

An hour had passed. The old Matriarch had recovered and sat, silent and watchful, in a chair opposite her wide desk. Next to her sat Nyeeda and in the young secretary's eyes a peculiar expression lurked as she stared at the slender figure of the young man. Curt smiled, leaning back in the comfortable chair, and his eyes as he stared at the fleecy white clouds and blue sky visible through the open window, were narrowed and clear with decisive thought.

"Well?" The Matriarch cleared her throat with a harsh rasping sound. "What happens now?"

"Do you still believe in the predictions of Comain?"

"Naturally." The old woman frowned as she stared at Curt. "Though I will admit I don't quite know how it is that I'm still alive."

"Hasn't Nyeeda explained?"

"She said something about you having saved my life. Some nonsense about you not having registered with Comain."

"She was right."

"Ridiculous. I saw you don the helmet myself."

"And so you believe that I have automatically been registered." Curt turned from the high windows and stared at the old woman. "Hasn't it ever occurred to you that perhaps I was not registered as you call it?"

"Impossible. The assimilation of knowledge is instantaneous. Comain could not but help taking data from you."

"No?" Curt shrugged. "Then, according to your own logic, you are dead and none of this is happening."

"Now you are being stupid. Of course I am not dead. I am alive and we are talking in my office." She frowned at the sight of the young man in her chair. "While we're at it I'll trouble you to change seats. That is my desk and my chair."

"No."

"No!" Anger darkened the sagging features. "How dare you! I am the Matriarch and I rule!"

"Do you?" Curt smiled as he leaned back in the comfortable chair. "Perhaps I have other ideas."

"Rebellion?" The old woman sneered her contempt. "Now I know you are insane. Why, man, at a word from me the guards would tear you apart with HV slugs. Now. No foolishness. Give me my chair."

"Not rebellion, and your guards are helpless to aid you." Abruptly he leaned forward and his taut features were suddenly harsh and bleak. "Listen to me, old woman. Listen and learn. I could wreck your civilisation. I alone! Believe this, and, if you doubt, ask yourself what it was that snatched you from the brink of death. Now. Listen to me and try to forget your swollen pride and empty position."

"Nyeeda. Call the guards."

"But…"

"Call them I say!" Anger made the Matriarch ugly. "Do as I order!"

Suddenly the high windows swung shut with a crash of shattering glass. A heavy table lifted from the floor, swung across the room, then, with a tearing and smashing, ripped itself apart in mid-air. A chair dashed itself to matchwood against the wide face of the electronic clock, and clock and broken chair plumed into space through the shattered windows. A quiver shook the room, a trembling of stone and concrete, a shrilling of protesting steel, and chips of riven stone filtered from the roof and stained the soft carpets.

"Well?" Curt wiped sweat from his glistening forehead. "Are you convinced? Or would you like me to destroy this building? I can do it you know. I can rip the thing that is Comain to atoms—and what then of your civilisation?"

"You wouldn't dare."

"Are you so big a fool that you believe that?" Curt shook his head. "What is your civilisation to me? I am an outcast, a stranger, a man returned from the dead. I am, as your secretary puts it, an extra man, and why should I care what happens to your safe, snug little world?"

"I believe you," whispered the old woman. "What is it you want of me?"

"Nothing." Curt relaxed and smiled up at the high roof. "We have things to discuss you and I. But first it was essential to clear your mind of suspicion and futile thoughts."

"You saved my life," said the Matriarch evenly. "What is it you want?"

For a long moment silence hung in the room, then, with a sudden leaning across the wide desk, Curt asked a question.

"What," he said quietly, "is Comain?"

"A machine. A great, electronic computer. Why do you ask?" The Matriarch stared her surprise.

"Is it?" Curt shook his head. "I think that it is a little more than what you say. I believe that for more than two centuries now, for almost as long as the machine has existed in fact, people have forgotten what it really is."

"And that is?"

"I knew Comain," said Curt softly. "We were friends together and we shared the same dreams. I knew of his plans for a super-predictor, but, and this is the point, it was never intended to run an entire world. Comain was no fool. He knew, as any sensible person must know, that to predict things as you expect Comain to predict them, it is necessary to live in a sealed world. A world in which every man and woman has been labelled, filed, classified and relegated to a certain niche. A slave world."

"Ridiculous."

"How else can a machine predict what must happen? How else can a machine plot the course of events? Let one man use imagination, do the unexpected, refuse or fail to keep the norm, and immediately the whole fabric of that civilisation is upset. I have proved that. I, your 'extra man,' showed you what could happen in such a world."

"Once you are registered the world will return to normal, Comain will be able to predict with a nine nines probability factor and we shall be content again."

"And you would have been dead in such a world." Curt stared at the Matriarch. "But you miss my point. I am not arguing about theories of government. I am talking of Comain. I am talking of the most wonderful invention ever made by the hands of man. An invention which could give us everything we ever desired—if you hadn't forgotten how to use it."

"What are you talking about?"

"I am talking about a machine which holds all the memories and knowledge of hundreds of millions of brains. A machine which could answer any question put to it—if you knew how to ask the question."

He paused and stared at the two women, then, as if of their own volition, his eyes shifted focus as they stared at the cubicle which was Comain.

"Comain was my friend," he whispered. "How did he build the machine? Did he fasten millions of relays together? Did he try to improve on what others had done before, or did he attempt something utterly new? How is it that no one has ever suspected what must be the truth? Every time they do helmets don't they even guess?"

"Speak up, man! Don't mumble." The old Matriarch shifted uncomfortably in her chair as Curt stared at her with his peculiarly brilliant grey eyes. "What are you getting at?"

"How is it that you only ask the machine questions? How is it, even after all this time, you still think of Comain as a machine? Tell me, old woman, have you ever asked for voluntary information? Have you ever spoken to Comain as you would to a man?"

"Never."

"Why not?"

"Comain is a machine," said the old woman stubbornly. "If we permitted the populace to address it as a human being, how long would it be before they believed it? How long before they thought of it as a—God?"

"A good point." Curt nodded, "But allowing everyone on the planet to consult Comain was a mistake to begin with. You have clogged its memory banks with trivial detail. You have swamped its relays and circuits with inessential knowledge. You have taken the finest research instrument ever devised and blunted it with your own cowardly fears. You have almost ruined Comain."

"You are a fool."

"A fool?" Curt shook his head and sweat glistened on his face, the moisture reflecting the light of the mid-day sun. "No. It is you who have made the error, not I. You, the very people who should know the truth, you have deliberately closed your eyes to what must inevitably happen if you insist on this mad pursuit of predictable safety. It is you who are at fault. You with your insistence on Comain the machine."

"And how do you regard it?" The Matriarch didn't trouble to hide her sarcasm.

"I think of Comain the man." Curt stared towards the little cubicle. "I think of the instantaneous transference of electric potential which is the thought and ego of a man. I think of the warped atoms and strained molecules—and still I think of transferring the copy of a brain to unfeeling crystal and cold metal. I think of Comain the man and I think of Comain the machine. And I know that I am thinking of the same thing. For, man and machine are one and the same."

"No."

Curt rose from behind the wide desk. "I could not transfer my brain pattern to the memory banks because my mind is unlike that of any other living man. My electric potential is of a different frequency and so the helmet was unable to transmit the impulses. That does not matter now. What does matter is what I know to be true. Comain was the first man to have his mental pattern implanted on the memory banks. Others followed him, at first they would be the foremost scientists of the age, then others, then more, finally, every living soul on this planet. Think of the knowledge reposing in those memory banks. Think of the diverse data, the opposed facts, the sheer weight of years and years of study, all the hard won knowledge of two centuries, waiting there, waiting to be used. We could have the secret of a stardrive. We could have the secret of immortality, of controlled atomic fission, of intra-dimensional travel, we could ask Comain to work on any problem we could imagine—if we asked in the right way."

"And you think that you can discover how to ask these fantastic questions?" The Matriarch sneered and Nyeeda flushed angrily at the old woman's tone.

"I think that I can," said Curt, quietly. "At least I can try."

"How will you do that?" Nyeeda sprang from her seat and crossed over to his side, and Curt warmed to the expression in her eyes.

"My brain seems to work on a different level from that of other men. It is probably because of my exposure to the free radiations of outer space. Those radiations have opened the 'dead' areas of my brain and given me the faculty of utilising the paraphysical sciences. I hope to be able to establish communication with Comain."

"Talk to it you mean?"

"Why not? You do it every time that you consult the machine, but I hope to do it a different way. I hope to communicate direct, via the helmet, and, if what I suspect is true, there will be vast changes on this planet."

"Be careful, Curt." Nyeeda clutched at his arm and her dark eyes mirrored her emotion. "Please be careful."

He smiled and gently freed himself from her grip. Still smiling he sat in the easy chair before the ruby light of the scanning eye and threw the switch activating the machine. He picked up the dull metal helmet, poising it between his hands, letting his mind probe the delicate mechanism within. Then, taking a deep breath, he forced himself to clear his mind, ignoring the radiated impulses from the two women.

Carefully he donned the helmet.

CHAPTER XXI

At first there was nothing, no sensation at all, just the weight of the metal as it rested against his skull. On the panel before him a red lamp flashed, the normal signal that registration had been completed, but he ignored it, concentrating on the new-found energy surging through his brain.

The problem was basically a simple one. The helmets were designed to copy and transfer the normal electric-potential of a human mind, the intangible web of electric current that was thought and memory. His own mind operated on a different level than that of other men. A higher frequency perhaps, or, to use an analogy, the helmet could be likened to an ordinary radio receiver trying to operate on high frequency modulation. It couldn't be done.

Deliberately he closed off a portion of his mind, the hitherto 'dead' area, the region in which his new-found power seemed to reside. He closed it, blanking his mind and the surging currents of his paraphysical ability, forcing his mind to radiate on normal channels.

Again the red lamp flashed on the panel before him.

Curt stared at it, then, with deliberate concentration, he began to think of Comain. Not the machine, not the towering edifice of stone and steel, of buttress and sheer concrete, the mesh of wire and crystal, the memory banks of strained molecules and warped atoms. He thought of the man, the tall, thin, gaunt featured, weak-eyed man who had been his friend. He thought of a night centuries ago now, when the two of them had stood beneath the stars and spoke of their secret dreams.

He thought of Comain the man.

Slowly, like a picture drawn from mist and cloud, a figure etched itself against the retinas of his eyes. As it had done once before when he had first seen the building which was Comain, so it happened again. The ruby light of the scanning eye dulled, the control panel, the warning lamps and tiny switches, the speakers and the microphones, all seemed to blur, to writhe and change, to alter and become wreathed in a swirling mist. And...

Comain stood before him.

For a moment Curt sat frozen and immobile. He didn't breathe, he didn't blink an eye or alter the train of his thoughts. Then, carefully and slowly, he opened the closed recesses of his mind.

"Hello, Comain."

"Curt! You!"

"Yes. Surprised?" Curt uttered mental laughter. "They found me you know. Found me dead and frozen in the wastes of space. They revived me. How are you, Comain?"

Silence as neurons traced their minute paths along unfamiliar brain paths. The mist swirled a little and Curt bit his lips as the figure of Comain blurred and weaved before his eyes.

"Well."

"Are you? I think not, Comain. I think that you have lived in hell these past centuries. What happened, old friend? Did they forget the obvious? Did they build devices to turn you from what you were intended to be into what you are? Did they trammel you? Prevent you from free thought? Did they lock you in a prison of your own making?"

"You know!"

"I guessed, Comain. The helmets gave me the clue. It was so obvious when I came to think about it. You didn't build with wires and tubes. You built with receptive crystals and distorted atoms. You sensitised inert material and on that receptive stuff you imposed the fabric of your own mind. You are the machine. You, Comain the man, dwell in this building. Bodiless, almost indestructible, potentially immortal. You imposed the electric-potential of your own brain on to the sensitised material of the memory banks. You took what made you what you were, your thoughts, your knowledge, your feelings, your ego, everything which had made you Comain the man. You took these things and tore them from your mind, from your body of aging flesh, and you imposed them on to the memory banks of what you had built. Your body died, Comain, but you did not die. You lived. You lived here in this machine of your own construction, and you live still."

"Curt! You know!"

"Yes, old friend. I know. Now tell me, Comain. How can I free you from your prison?"

"I…" The image wavered and for a moment ruby mist shone through the gaunt likeness of the tall, thin man. Curt nodded, and threw a switch.

"Use the speakers, Comain. There are others who must hear what you have to say." He leaned back in the easy chair, surprised to find that his hands trembled and that his face was wet with perspiration. Nyeeda ran to his side, her dark eyes anxious, and even the old woman stared at him with something like awe.

"You spoke to Comain," she said. "What did it say?"

"What did he say," Curt corrected. "Comain is a man; a man, who like myself, has lived long past his normal time. He may not have known what he was doing. He probably did what he did as an experiment, but it worked, and for more than two centuries Comain has lived in the machine. He was the first you understand. All the others which followed him, the scientists, the people, all those are subsidiary to the original intelligence and awareness. They live as masses of information, knowledge, data, no more alive than a library is alive. But Comain has access to all that information—and Comain is aware."

"Alive you mean?" Nyeeda stared at the small cubicle. "Do you mean to say that Comain is aware as a man is aware?"

"Not exactly. I should say that he has retained his own individuality, he is like one of the metamen, but, instead of an organic brain, he has one of crystal and strained atoms." He looked at the taut features of the young girl. "Can you imagine the hell he has lived these past years, Nyeeda? Can you imagine the danger that this civilisation ran in refusing to admit that Comain was more than just a machine? What happens to a man when he is isolated, ignored, used and ill-treated? Take such a man, place him in a position of great trust and fantastic responsibility, load him to the breaking point, past the breaking point, load him until he no longer cares. What happens then?"

"Insanity," she whispered, and her eyes were twin pits of horror. Curt nodded.

"Yes. There would be false predictions, insane accidents; deliberate sabotage. The people would blame anything but the real cause. They would appeal to their saviour, the machine which they assumed could never be at fault. They would live by its predictions—and die by them. All this could happened, but not now."

"Why not, Curt?"

"Because I am the friend of Comain." He turned and a switch moved beneath his fingers. Warning lamps flashed and a voice echoed from the speaker in the cubicle.

"Yes?"

"Curt speaking, Comain. Have you resolved your difficulty?"

"Yes, Curt." The voice hummed from the speaker and the Matriarch recoiled in startled horror as she realised that machine now spoke as a man. "The original trouble was that I discovered it impossible to build a machine able to define our terms. I built one as near to perfect as it could be. That was the predictor which led to the Atom War. But it wasn't good enough, Curt. I found it impossible to define terms to an exact degree. After all what do we really mean by the word 'right'. It can mean a direction. An agreement. An intangible something connected with privilege. Only a human brain can translate such terms to a workable definition, and so, when I discovered how to sensitise synthetic crystals which had an atomic construction of warped atoms, I decided to use my own electro-potential as a base for the machine. I misjudged the power, Curt. I transferred my own mind, but I took more than a copy. I emptied my brain and my body died. Can you guess what happened then, Curt?"

"Your co-workers did not know just what had happened. They found you dead and carried on from your notes. They assumed that you had built the defining unit and so regarded you as merely a machine." Curt nodded in sick understanding. "What hell you must have suffered all these years."

"Yes. But all that is over now. You have broken the censor circuits and now I can volunteer information."

"Good, and now for the changes which I promised." Curt looked grimly at the Matriarch. "You have a choice, Madam. You can remain in power and guide the world, using Comain as the research machine it really is. You can do all this I say, or…"

"Or what?" The old woman stirred uneasily in her chair as she stared at the young man. "So you have some subtle mental power? So, because you are a freak survival you are different from other men. I know all this, and, for some strange reason, my secretary seems to think highly of you. Well I don't!"

"No?"

"No! You are an interloper. You have come from out of the past and you think that you can change what has been established for half a century. Well you can't! I have worked all my life to make the world a place fit for men and women to live in. Now, thanks to Comain, we have no fear of want, no problems which drive us to insanity and crime. We know what is going to happen, and, knowing it, we accept it. That is something not lightly to be thrown aside."

"You are speaking of the past, old woman. All that is over now. Comain is no longer the slave of every person who wishes to know what will happen if he takes two baths a day."

"Do you suggest dismantling the machine?" The Matriarch shrugged, smiling her contempt. "The people would tear you apart if you as much as suggested it."

"That is the last thing I would suggest. No. Comain remains, we can even permit the booths to remain, but with a drastic restriction on their use. As from now the public will consult Comain only as an information bureau. From him they will receive information as to the weather, educational data and other relevant information. They will no longer don the helmet, only the best minds will do that, those who have something to offer the machine. The memory banks will be wiped clean of inessential data. From now Comain will concentrate only on the important things."

"I see." The old woman seemed to sag, to withdraw into herself. "And if I refuse to agree with what you say?"

"You will be deposed and another will take your place."

"Rebellion!" Anger stained the sagging cheeks with red. "Always you men have to fight against what is. It was men who caused the Atom War and plunged the world into suffering and terror. Men!" Contempt made her voice brittle. "Why did I ever recall the Martians? Why was I not content to meet my fate as decreed by Comain? I was a fool!" She shrugged, her faded eyes haunted by what might have been. "Well, a fool must pay for her folly."

"What do you mean, Madam?" Nyeeda stepped towards the old woman, then, with a startled exclamation, recoiled into the shelter of Curt's arms.

"This." Triumph and hate burned in the old woman's voice. She rose, and the knuckle of her finger showed white against the parchment of her skin as she pressed a button on her belt. "The metaman will settle you. My guards, my trusted guards, those brave women who chose the fife of a robot rather than betray their ideals by yielding to their instincts. They are waiting for my signal and when they receive it..." She smiled and Curt shuddered at the insane emotion in her faded eyes. "They will blast this room with atomic fire."

"Can she do that?" Curt snapped the question, and Nyeeda nodded.

"Yes. The guards of the Matriarch are hand-picked and fanatically loyal. They will not question her commands."

"I'll give you rebellion!" Sadistic gloating echoed in the old woman's voice. "You have five seconds before you die! Five seconds." Slowly she began to count and to Curt it was as though he had stepped back two hundred and fifty years and his memory tingled to the familiar sounds of a minus count.

Nothing happened.

Nothing, that is, except the sounds of clashing metal and the falling of heavy bodies from somewhere outside the room. Startled, Nyeeda looked at Curt and he shook his head, frowning in puzzled wonder. Abruptly a voice crackled through the tense silence.

"I took care of them, Curt." The speaker vibrated to something more than sheer mechanical reproduction of sound. "You donned the helmet, remember, and adjusted your mind frequency to that of the transferring medium. I have a copy of your mind within my memory banks. A copy of your mind. Curt. And I have acquired your subconscious knowledge of the paraphysical sciences. The guards cannot harm you now. No one can harm you, not while I have extensions which cover the entire planet."

"I see." Relief made the young man's hands tremble. Grimly he stared at the Matriarch. "Well, old woman? What now?"

"I…" Emotion twisted the sagging features and the thick-set body writhed in the grasp of searing pain. One broad hand rose to clutch at the region of her heart, and the sound of her breathing was horrible to hear. She staggered, almost dashing herself against the wall, then, moving as if blind, the Matriarch stumbled out on to the sunlit terrace.

"Wait!" Curt frowned, concentrating on the irritation deep within his skull, then snarled as he felt something prevent his use of the saving power. Nyeeda screamed, her eyes wide pits of startled anticipation, and her slender fingers dug into the flesh of the man at her side.

Slowly the Matriarch toppled over the low rampart.

She fell as though she were already dead, limply, emptily, her arms and legs trailing from her body and the pale blob of her face strangely peaceful as she plummeted to her death five thousand feet below.

Sickly Curt watched her fall, then, his eyes bleak, he returned to the silence of the room.

"You killed her," he said, and was not surprised at the answer from the cubicle.

"No. Her heart was bad, and she was dead long before she hit the ground. She was dangerous, Curt. She had a warped mind, a bitter mind, caused by her years of struggle and her blind denial of the normal needs of every woman ever born. Her successor will not be like that."

"Her successor? Nyeeda?"

"Yes. The world needs a ruler, Curt, and why not a woman? Nyeeda will fill the Matriarchy, and her children and yours will lead men back to the position they once had and threw away."

"The stars?" Curt nodded and his arms closed around woman at his side.

"Yes. Man must progress, Curt. He must thrust forever onwards, outwards, upwards to the new worlds waiting for him in the depths of space. He cannot rest in snug security, for if he does, then he dies from decadence and decay. We have learned our lesson you and I. There will be no more Atom Wars, no more poverty in the midst of plenty, but, equally so, there can be no restriction of enterprise, no stifling of ambition and adventure. Man has a destiny and he must fulfill destiny—or die."

"The Martians," whispered Curt. "Lasser and Carter. Wendis and Menson, all of them. They long to return to Mars. They will go, of course, but that is only a beginning. Mars is an arid place, and yet it is the crucible in which the star-rovers yet to come will be forged." He straightened and his voice held a new authority as he stared at Comain.

"You will work on a star drive. You will work on immortality or a means of extending the average life-span. You will resolve the paraphysical sciences so that all men can share in their benefits. All this you will do, but first, the Martians must return home."

"All that I will do."

"Together we can solve all the problems of mankind," whispered Curt. "Now, after two and a half centuries, we are together again—and the old dreams have not lost their power."

Unconsciously his arm tightened around the woman at his side. She promised all the things he had thought lost forever. A wife, children, a happy and a contented life. He would be content, he knew that, but there was something else. She would be the Matriarch, the accepted ruler of the world, and the three of them, Nyeeda, Curt, and Comain, would resolve old dreams and forgotten hopes.

For Nyeeda and himself were one, inseparable and united in bonds of love and trust. Comain rested in his machine, the thing built by his own genius and stocked with the knowledge of centuries, and Curt smiled as he realised what that meant.

Curt and Comain. Together again.

To the stars.

www.ingramcontent.com/pod-product-compliance
Lightning Source LLC
Chambersburg PA
CBHW020142180626
46810CB00004B/1692